Brer Anansi's
LUCKY ESCAPE
and other stories

Brer Anansi's
LUCKY ESCAPE
and other stories

by David P Makhanlall

illustrated by Ant Parker

Blackie Children's Books

BLACKIE CHILDREN'S BOOKS

Published by the Penguin Group
Penguin Books Ltd, 27 Wrights Lane, London W8 5TZ, England
Penguin Books USA Inc., 375 Hudson Street, New York, New York 10014, USA
Penguin Books Australia Ltd, Ringwood, Victoria, Australia
Penguin Books Canada Ltd, 10 Alcorn Avenue, Toronto, Ontario, Canada M4V 3B2
Penguin Books (NZ) Ltd, 182-190 Wairau Road, Auckland 10, New Zealand

Penguin Books Ltd, Registered Offices: Harmondsworth, Middlesex, England

First published 1992
10 9 8 7 6 5 4 3 2 1

Text copyright © David P Makhanlall 1992
Illustration © Ant Parker 1992

The moral right of the author/illustrator has been asserted

Printed in Great Britain

A CIP catalogue record for this book is available from the British Library

ISBN 0 216 93217 3

To my boys, Michael and Kevin,
from Daddy.
Always willing, always there.

Contents

Introduction

During long summer holidays and early evenings, the children of the village would gather on the old woman's steps. She would dazzle them with tales of the old country where animals were brave and extraordinarily intelligent and roamed the earth as kings among men.

The children, all barefoot and wide-eyed, would listen in awe at the stories. Of all the heroes in the stories, the most famous is *Buru Nansi*, long famous for his cunning, trickery and ability to outlast all the other heroes. Through tale after tale, Brer Anansi has survived. He is more refined, up-to-date, colourful and he has learned to live dangerously. He is a survivor and he will always survive.

The name Anansi itself is of West African origin, the name of the god of trickery and deceit. To be called a Brer ('brother') god among the animals signifies his ability to always be on the look-out. He is not wicked for the sake of it; indeed, he outsmarts those who are out to destroy his character and his credibility, and he sometimes wins by pure luck.

Agee Mai (meaning great grandmother, the teller of tales) would limit the evenings to only one Anansi story. Sometimes the story sittings, two or three times a week, would last until nine or ten in the evening. Many of the younger children would fall asleep long before this, but the older ones were intrigued. In the evenings, Brer Anansi came alive for the children. Their imaginations took hold and, in the pale moonlight, Brer Anansi seemed to be in the dark corner of the storyteller's room, making sure not a word was missing from the tale.

Also in schools, the younger children of up to nine or ten years would sharpen their reading skills with simple Anansi tales in the school readers. There, the tales were simple and direct and served to whet the appetite of the active and eager.

The Big Slap is a story I first heard when I was eight or nine and I have heard it so many times, I could never forget it. It is certainly my favourite Brer Anansi story and one I did not put into writing until I was eighteen or so. The highlight of the story for me was whether the door would be opened and the guest would collect the milk. At this particular point, the silence was heavy and the sight of the children's open mouths and wide unblinking eyes was incredible.

The Lucky Escape is yet another story where Anansi in his absence causes problems for his enemies, then innocently returns, not in the least aware of what has happened, what is happening or what is going to happen. In this story Anansi, who is thought to be dead, turns up carrying a post. This is one of the oldest and best of the Anansi stories, full of danger and excitement, fun and intrigue, and every time it is retold it gains more flavour. It is one of the more unusual stories, in that there are several high-points of laughter and excitement, all seeming to start from a string of apparent coincidences.

So read on! Let the stories come alive. Imagine it is late evening and the moon has just come up to play skipping-rope among the young stars, and you are eight or ten, hanging on every word. Imagine some parent creeping up from behind to collect their child, whispering ANANSI and the children shrieking and jumping up from the makeshift benches that are Agee Mai's house steps. Read on!

D.M.

9

Smartest Animal of the Year

Every year all the animals of the forest gathered together to find out which of them was the Smartest Animal of the Year. Brer Rabbit had won the title for three years in succession. Brer Anansi had never won, so this year he was more determined than ever to win.

Brer Bear had won five years ago and as prize he received a dozen jars of honey, ten pounds of pure sugar and a barrel of syrup. For each of the three years he was chosen, Brer Rabbit received a barrow full of carrots, two bags of peaches and a sack of plums. If I win, thought Brer Anansi, I will get five bunches of plantains, two sacks of yams and fifty pounds of potatoes; I must win. The first thing to do, he decided, was to bribe the judges.

The chief judge was Leo the lion, King of all the animals. Brer Anansi decided to present him with a gift.

Brer Anansi knew that Leo's favourite dish was roast chicken with plenty of potatoes and butter, so he went to see Mr. Hawk. By telling him that he would get half the money the King would give for the gift, Brer Anansi persuaded him to go and catch a fat chicken from Mr. Brown's chicken pen. Mr. Hawk soon returned with a nice, plump chicken.

Brer Anansi next went to see the White Swan. He praised her cooking to the skies, telling her she was the best cook in all the land. Soon the chicken was roasting away on the fire. But Brer Anansi had only three potatoes with him, and such a large chicken would need at least six. What was worse, he hadn't any butter.

But who could he ask? None of the other animals were likely to give him any butter or potatoes. They never lent him anything because he never returned what they did lend him. He decided, all the same, to ask Brer Rabbit for some potatoes and a pound of butter. You never can tell, he thought, he just might lend them to me.

He went up to Brer Rabbit's burrow and knocked on the door. Brer Rabbit popped out his head.

'Well, Brer Anansi, what do you want?'

'Good morning, Brer Rabbit. I am wondering if you can lend me three potatoes, just three.'

'Potatoes?' snapped Brer Rabbit. 'What do you want with potatoes?'

'You see, I am sick and I want to make some mashed potatoes. I can't go to the fields to get any.'

'Steal any, you mean. I can't lend you any,' said Brer Rabbit firmly.

Brer Anansi pretended to be sad. He turned away slowly with tears in his eyes.

Brer Rabbit was not nearly as hard-hearted as he sounded. He only pretended to be fierce to keep all that he had to himself.

'Come back here, Brer Anansi,' he called. 'I will lend you three potatoes. Only three, mind you.'

'Oh, thank you, Brer Rabbit. Thank you so much. But please give me a pound of butter too, or at least some.'

Brer Rabbit fetched the three potatoes and a small paper dish filled with butter. He presented them to Brer Anansi and watched as he walked away with them. Brer Rabbit hadn't been the Smartest Animal of the Year for three years for nothing. He smelt a rat. Brer Anansi never liked butter yet he borrowed a pound!

The rabbit followed at a safe distance behind the spider. Soon they came in sight of the White Swan's house. Brer Rabbit raised his eyebrows in wonder. He was even more surprised when he saw the huge chicken roasting on the fire. He hid outside and peered through the window. He could hear all that went on inside.

'Ah,' said Brer Anansi when he smelt the molten butter that the White Swan poured over the roast chicken, 'the King will surely be happy with this gift!'

King? Brer Rabbit was puzzled. Now why would Brer Anansi be presenting the King with a gift? Brer Rabbit knew that Brer Anansi never gave anything away for nothing. 'Unless—wait, I've got it,' he said. 'The big contest is in a week's time: he wants to be the Smartest Animal of the Year. But he won't be if I can help it.'

Brer Rabbit hurried away as quickly as he could. He was going to tell the King what Brer Anansi was up to.

An hour later, Brer Anansi took his gift to the King. He did not know that Brer Rabbit was aware of his plan. The King pretended not to know what was going on. He took the chicken and potatoes and set about eating them immediately.

Between mouthfuls, he said to Brer Anansi, 'Now, Brer Anansi, I must thank you for this gift. Remember, if there is anything you want, just ask me.'

Brer Anansi's heart was beating fast. Quietly he said, 'Yes, King, I want to know if my name is among the three animals who were selected to take part this year in the Smartest Animal of the Year contest.'

'Oh-ho, is that so!' chuckled the lion, smacking his lips and licking the butter that dribbled down his golden mane. 'I will tell you. Yes, I will tell you. You are in the list, but you are number three. Brer Rabbit is first and Brer Bear is second, so you have a lot of catching up to do in the final contest. Mind you, I cannot do anything to help you.'

The lion rolled his tongue about and swallowed a potato in one gulp!

Brer Anansi left quickly. He was sad, very sad. He walked slowly home. If Brer Rabbit did not win, then Brer Bear was sure to win.

He saw Brer Rabbit a good hundred yards away waiting for him. There was a wide grin on his face. 'So he told the King about my plan,' grumbled Brer Anansi. The rogue! But he was not beaten yet. He had another plan.

Brer Anansi straightened up and put on a wider grin than Brer Rabbit's.

'Say, Brer Anansi, you look pleased about something. What did the King tell you?'

'Ah, Brer Rabbit. If you only knew, my friend. The King

14

was pleased with me. He told me which animals are in the finals next week. I am in the list, of course, and so is Brer Bear, and you too. But I am sure of winning!'

Now Brer Rabbit was consumed with curiosity to know what was going on.

'Come on, friend,' said Brer Rabbit, clapping Brer Anansi on the back. 'I am the one who lent you the potatoes and butter. Now suppose you tell me why you are so sure that you will win.'

'Easy,' said Brer Anansi with a smile. 'The King told me the questions we will be getting next week. I know all the questions but only some of the answers.'

Brer Rabbit was too smart to give up that easily, though he was naturally disappointed that the King had told Brer Anansi all the questions and had not told them to him. The rabbit eagerly asked Brer Anansi what the questions were.

Brer Anansi pretended to be reluctant to tell, but after getting a barrow full of potatoes and a bunch of plantains, he told the rabbit the questions.

'But those are last year's questions,' said Brer Rabbit.

'Of course they are. Do you remember the answers?'

'No,' replied Brer Rabbit, scratching his head.

'Then you had better find them out. The King knew we wouldn't remember the answers so he set the same questions again. You better go and prepare them.'

Brer Rabbit ran into his burrow as fast as he could. It didn't even occur to him that Brer Anansi would fool him. He wouldn't dare. He intended to prepare the questions!

Brer Anansi smiled. Now only he or Brer Bear was likely to win. He had given Brer Rabbit the wrong questions. Even Brer Anansi didn't know the correct ones. The rabbit was going to be awfully disappointed.

Next Brer Anansi went to see Brer Bear. He was going to try and fool him too. He found Brer Bear chopping wood in

15

his back-yard. He was very angry that he had wood to chop.

'Good morning, Brer Bear,' said Brer Anansi. 'I have news for you.'

'What news?' asked Brer Bear. 'Are you going to return the honey I lent you last year?'

'No, no. I have much more important news. It is about the contest that is coming up in a week from now. Brer Rabbit went to see the King and guess what? He was given the questions to this year's contest!'

'What?' Brer Bear was so excited that he nearly sliced his own foot with the sharp axe.

'Yes, it's true. Why don't you go and see for yourself?'

'I will do just that,' said Brer Bear and he dashed off to see Brer Rabbit without even locking his kitchen door. When he was out of sight, Brer Anansi helped himself to two jars of honey from the kitchen, and was soon whistling his way homewards. His plan had worked perfectly so far.

The week flew past. Saturday arrived and all the animals were gathered in Farmer Brown's empty cornfield. The farmer was away at the market so they were safe for the time being.

The three chosen animals were given chairs in the centre of the ring formed by the other animals. Brer Rabbit was all smiles. He had a large tag on his shirt. On it was written *number one*. He was sure to win, he thought. Brer Bear too was all smiles. His card read *number two*. He was sure of winning! Brer Bear had crept into Brer Rabbit's burrow when the rabbit had gone to borrow a dictionary from the Bookworm. He found the list of questions that Brer Rabbit had written down and he copied them. The he rubbed out the last question on Brer Rabbit's list and substituted one from his head. Brer Rabbit then had one wrong question without knowing it.

16

Paper and pencil was given to each contestant, together with a list of questions. The King rang his bell and the contest started.

Brer Rabbit did not even bother to read the questions. He quickly wrote down all the answers he had prepared. Brer Bear did the same thing. He wanted to finish first!

Brer Anansi took his time. He read every question carefully and wrote down what he thought were the correct answers.

Of course, Brer Rabbit finished first. Brer Bear was second and Brer Anansi was last. The King had to snatch away Brer Anansi's paper as the time for answering was up.

The owl examined the answers carefully. The King was soon handed the results.

'Ahem,' said the King. 'Brer Rabbit finished his questions first, but he wrote last year's answers to this year's questions. He didn't even get all of them correct! He would have failed even if he had got them all correct!'

Brer Rabbit could hardly believe his ears. 'Me, Brer Rabbit, failed!' he gasped. He looked at Brer Anansi and ground his teeth together. The rogue!

'Now, for Brer Bear's answers,' said the King. 'At least he did better than Brer Rabbit. He got all last year's answers correct. He has failed!'

Brer Bear looked at Brer Rabbit and smacked his lips. 'I am going to eat him,' he growled under his breath.

'Now for the final contestant's results,' said the King. 'Brer Anansi has got one answer correct. He is the Smartest Animal of the Year! Hooray for Brer Anansi!'

Brer Anansi was greeted with cheers from the other animals. He came up for his prize but did not collect it. He saw the look on Brer Bear's face and Brer Rabbit's ugly grin. He knew that he had some running to do!

17

He told the King to keep his prize for him, and took to his heels with Brer Bear and Brer Rabbit snorting behind. He reached his house and pulled up the silk rope that led down to the ground. He was safe. Brer Bear and Brer Rabbit could not climb up after him. They waited below.

'You just come down here, Brer Anansi,' said Brer Bear, 'and we will show you where barley grows!'

But Brer Anansi did not mind. He knew that Brer Bear and Brer Rabbit would soon get hungry and leave him alone. Besides, he could wait in his house for as long as a month. He had two jars of honey, a barrow of potatoes and a bunch of plantains to live on.

What was more, he was the Smartest Animal of the Year too!

The Gold Rush

One day, when Brer Anansi was thinking about the ways in which he could become rich, Brer Bear came up to him. Normally, Brer Bear would have chased Brer Anansi as soon as he saw him but this time he had a good reason for not doing so. He had one of his big plans!

'Hello, Brer Anansi,' said Brer Bear. 'What are you thinking about?'

Brer Anansi looked up slowly at Brer Bear. 'You know what, Brer Bear?' he said. 'I am wondering what would happen if I became rich. Own a gold mine or something, you know.'

'Become rich!' exclaimed Brer Bear. 'Why, man, everyone would respect you. You would be called Baron Anansi. Even King Leo would respect you!'

'Ah, my friend,' said Brer Anansi, sadly, 'that can never come to pass. How should a poor Brer Anansi like me become rich?'

Brer Bear took out a small piece of paper from his pocket and showed it to Brer Anansi.

'Here, friend, this is a map. A map of a gold mine.'

'A gold what?' shouted Brer Anansi, jumping up from the log he was sitting on. 'How did you get it?'

'I can't tell you that. Just say that I found it outside Brer Rabbit's house. The wind must have blown it out of his window. Here, have a closer look.'

Brer Anansi looked at the map closely. It showed every detail. The mine was marked with an X. Brer Anansi looked keenly at every landmark on the map. He knew where the mine was! It was not far from an old well he knew about. He pretended to lose interest in the map.

'Aw, it's no good. It is a fake map,' said Brer Anansi.

Just then Brer Rabbit came up. He was very angry. Someone had stolen his map! He saw Brer Bear with the map, and stamped his feet and ground his teeth.

'You thief! What do you mean by stealing my map, Brer Bear?'

'Of course I did not steal your map, Brer Rabbit. I found it outside your burrow.'

'A likely story!' shouted back Brer Rabbit.

While the two were arguing, Brer Anansi ran home as fast as he could. He was going to dig for the gold mine! He quickly climbed up the silk rope that led to his house and was soon down with a spade. He hurried off to the old well.

Five minutes later Brer Bear stopped arguing with Brer Rabbit, and looked around. There was no sign of Brer Anansi!

'Where is Brer Anansi?' asked Brer Bear.

'Who wants to know where he is?' replied Brer Rabbit. 'You would want to know, if I told you he has seen the map.'

'Brer Anansi has seen the map?' repeated the smart Brer Rabbit. 'Why, I bet he is over there right now digging. Come on, get your spade and let's go.'

The two hurried quickly towards the old well, following the map all the way. They only stopped at Brer Bear's house to collect a spade. Soon they came in sight of the old well. Brer Anansi was there and he was digging furiously!

Brer Bear and Brer Rabbit hid in the bushes nearby and looked on.

'When he finds the treasure,' said Brer Rabbit, 'we will throw him down the old well and take all the gold. Of course, the gold is all mine, but I will give you half of it if you help me deal with Brer Anansi.'

'Yes, yes, I agree,' replied Brer Bear.

Brer Anansi was not aware that his two enemies were looking on. He thought that he was all alone and dug away as fast as he could. He wanted to find the treasure all by himself before those two rogues came and took it for themselves. The ground was hard and the digging was difficult. How Brer Anansi sweated!

His two enemies just chuckled and looked on. Everytime Brer Anansi stopped to wipe the sweat from his face, Brer Bear nudged his friend and smiled.

'He is getting tired,' said Brer Rabbit. 'He'd better find the treasure quickly or he will die of exhaustion.'

Brer Anansi dug on. Indeed, he was getting tired, but he had to continue digging. He wanted to be a baron, and a rich one at that.

At last his spade struck something solid, with a clang. When Brer Bear and Brer Rabbit heard that, they both scrambled up and ran towards Brer Anansi. Brer Bear lifted Brer Anansi with one hand and threw him down the well!

The two looked into the hole Brer Anansi had been digging. There was something there, all right. Brer Rabbit took his spade and cleared away the dirt.

'There is nothing here but old tins,' said Brer Rabbit.

'Then the gold mine is still here somewhere. We were too hasty in throwing Brer Anansi down the well. Let's see if we can get him out of there and let him dig again until he finds it.'

But they could not get Brer Anansi out of the well. It was far too deep for Brer Anansi to climb out and there was no rope around to help him. He was trapped. But he had made an important discovery inside the well!

'Come on,' said Brer Rabbit. 'I will help you dig. You use your spade and I will use Brer Anansi's.'

'Yes, we will get the gold mine all for ourselves. It is a lucky thing for Brer Anansi that there isn't any water in the well or he would have drowned. He doesn't like water.'

Brer Rabbit and Brer Bear began to dig away at top speed. In half-an-hour they had dug up all the ground on the right side of the well, and still there was no gold mine to be seen. Not even a speck of gold dust!

'I know what,' said Brer Rabbit. 'The animal who drew the map must have placed the X on the wrong side of the well. Let's dig over there.'

So they took up their spades and went to the other side of the well to dig. The earth was even harder on that side and Brer Bear was getting angry.

'Brer Rabbit,' he asked, 'where did you get this map from?'

'Brer Buzzard gave it to me. He said he found it in a prospector's hut near the mountains. It is genuine, I am sure. We will get the treasure soon.'

'We'd better!' said Brer Bear, looking steadily at Brer Rabbit.

The two heroes dug almost every inch of the ground around the well and still there were no signs of a gold mine. They were so keen on their digging that they failed to see Farmer Brown creeping steadily closer through the bushes. He had his gun with him.

'I have caught you red-handed this time, you rascals! Digging up my land!'

Brer Rabbit and Brer Bear jumped high into the air in fright. When they came down to the ground again, they ran for their lives. Farmer Brown was after them, his double-barrel gun at the ready.

Brer Anansi listened to all that went on from inside the well. Good, he said, my two enemies are gone for good, but how am I going to get out of this well? He waited until Farmer Brown came back, and then he cried in a weak voice:

'Farmer Brown, Farmer Brown, those two rogues threw me in here when they saw that I was going to tell you that they were digging up your land.'

Farmer Brown looked down into the well. 'Digging up my land! I wanted to plant some tomatoes here, and they saved me the trouble of digging up this land all by myself. If you had come and warned me, I would have chased them away long ago. But since you didn't, I will get you out. Wait, and I'll go and get a ladder.'

The farmer soon returned with a ladder and lowered it down the well.

'You can come out and leave the ladder here. I am going to get some tomato seeds from the store.'

Brer Anansi hurried out and ran home for his barrow. He was rich, after all. Quickly he ran back to the old well and climbed down again. In no time at all, he had half a barrow of gold coins!

The old well was really a wishing well and animals used to go there and throw in a coin and make a wish. Brer Anansi smiled as he wheeled his barrow home. His two lazy friends had worked hard for nothing. Farmer Brown was pleased with Brer Anansi because he had helped to dig up his land to plant tomatoes. Brer Anansi had enough gold coins to buy anything. Brer Bear and Brer Rabbit had only bruises to show for their scheming.

The Big Slap

One morning Brer Anansi woke up feeling very happy. He had had a good night's sleep and felt as if he could pull up a tree from the ground with all its roots and branches. So after he ate his breakfast he went in search of adventure.

Not long after he left home the sky became cloudy and it was soon a bit dark. Then Mr. Thunder was heard. He roared and tumbled in the skies. Now why is he making all that noise, thought Brer Anansi. Mr. Thunder doesn't seem to know that I'm around. I had better tell him.

Raising his voice, he shouted, 'Ho, there Thunder! How dare you make all that noise when I am around? Don't you have any respect for me?'

Mr. Thunder was furious. He had never been called simply Thunder in his entire life. He was always addressed as Mr. Thunder. It made him even more furious that a spider should dare to ask him to show respect. Why should the big, strong Mr. Thunder respect an overgrown spider?

Mr. Thunder roared so loudly that the earth shook and the leaves fell off the trees as if autumn was in full swing. But Brer Anansi was not the least bit afraid. He considered himself to be a very brave spider, the only brave spider in the world!

'Anansi!' shouted Mr. Thunder. 'Who are you to demand respect from me? You—only a spider! How dare you question my roaring? Just you tell me who you think you are!'

Brer Anansi was now very, very angry. How dare Thunder speak to him like that! I will put him in his place, he thought. Big mouthed fellow!

'You are nothing but a wind-bag, Thunder. You can frighten all the other animals but not me!' said Brer Anansi and stamped his many feet on the ground.

'Is that so, Anansi?' asked Mr. Thunder. 'Are you mad? If I slapped you, your head would fall off and roll miles and miles away. You would be searching for a long time for it. Ha-ha!'

'What?' Brer Anansi was purple with rage. 'I will show you. I can take a slap from you. Know what? You call tomorrow morning at my house at four o'clock and I will take a slap from you. Do you think you are brave enough to come to my house?'

'Come to your house!' roared Mr. Thunder. 'I will do worse than that. I will do much worse. I will slap your head off. I will come tomorrow morning and do just that!'

And Mr. Thunder gave a final long and loud roar that shook the clouds and made the rain pour down in gallons. Brer Anansi was wet right down to his toes. Now water was a thing that Brer Anansi did not like, so he ran home as fast as he could. He was shaking like a leaf in a strong wind.

As he dried himself near his fire, Brer Anansi remembered what he had told Mr. Thunder. Now he was afraid. He had challenged Mr. Thunder to slap him dead, and sure enough Mr. Thunder would slap him dead.

He was in a really tight fix this time. It was very foolish of him to argue with Mr. Thunder. Brer Anansi sat on his bed with his chin in his hands. He was very sad. Tomorrow he was going to die!

Then Brer Anansi had an idea. A very good idea. It might just work, he thought, or else he would be a dead spider. He immediately dashed outside and ran down the road to where Brer Cock lived.

'Oh, my dear friend, Brer Cock!' said Brer Anansi. 'It has been a long time since I saw you last. How about having dinner with me? Come on, I will give you rum too. How about that!'

Brer Cock was interested. He liked rum a lot so he went to have dinner with Brer Anansi.

They had a wonderful time. There were roasted plantains, tinned beans and plenty of rum. Brer Anansi, of course, had stolen all this the day before from the store. Brer Cock really enjoyed himself. At last, he was ready to leave.

'Oh, why don't you spend the night with me? We can play cards and talk most of the night!'

There was some rum left so Brer Cock stayed. But Brer

Anansi had a favour to ask.

'Brer Cock,' he said, 'I am not an early riser, so I am wondering if you can collect the milk for me. The delivery comes at four and you only have to show your face at the door when it comes.'

'I will do that,' replied Brer Cock. 'I am an earlier riser than the sun. Have no fear, I will collect the milk.'

Brer Anansi was happy. He had found a solution to his problems.

The next morning Brer Anansi was not afraid, nor was he asleep. It was almost four o'clock and he was waiting to see what would happen. Sure enough, there was a loud rapping at the door. The nails on the door rattled. Now Brer Anansi was becoming afraid. Brer Cock heard the rapping and remembered about the delivery. He opened the door and poked his head out.

What a slap he got! Ten seconds later, Brer Cock lay dead on the floor.

'Aha,' Mr. Thunder said, 'that took care of you!' and he growled loudly as he walked home. It had been too dark for him to see that it was not Brer Anansi who answered the door.

After his footsteps had died away, Brer Anansi got up and began preparing Brer Cock for the pot. By seven in the morning he had a stewed cock all ready to be eaten. But first he went to see Mr. Thunder.

What a surprise Mr. Thunder got!

'You are not dead? Are you really alive? I must have slapped you too lightly. How about another slap tomorrow morning?'

Brer Anansi felt so brave and proud that he accepted. He went home feeling very happy. He would use the same trick again.

This time his guest was Brer Tiger. Now Brer Tiger liked meat a lot so he gladly went to dinner with Brer Anansi. The cock was well-cooked and the tiger had a feast. When it was time to leave Brer Anansi produced the half-bottle of rum he had hidden the night before from Brer Cock. Brer Tiger decided without much fuss to spend the night. Eventually, Brer Tiger was told the milk delivery story, and he agreed—unfortunately for him—to collect the milk. He did not know that Brer Anansi never drank milk.

The following morning at four o'clock, Brer Tiger heard the knock on the door. Out came his head, and—POW! What a slap he got! In five seconds he lay dead. The slap was much harder than the one Brer Cock had received.

Brer Anansi soon buried Brer Tiger in his backyard. When it was light enough he went to see Mr. Thunder.

Mr. Thunder was even more furious than before. He stamped and snorted and growled and hissed. Finally, after a lot of fuming, he quietened down when Brer Anansi agreed to a third and final slap.

Brer Anansi went to invite his third guest. The clever spider told everyone how he had killed Mr. Tiger with his bare hands. Mr. Leopard was no friend of Brer Tiger. When he heard that Brer Anansi had killed him he gladly went to dinner with Brer Anansi.

After dinner, Brer Anansi told the milk delivery story for the third time. Mr. Leopard was no fool. He knew that Brer Anansi never drank milk, but still, he pretended to agree to collect the milk.

Brer Anansi was happy. He thought that he was going to fool Mr. Leopard. But he was mistaken, for as soon as he had dropped off to sleep, Mr. Leopard crept outside and hid up a tree.

Four o'clock came and there was the usual rapping. Brer

Anansi smiled to himself. Mr. Leopard would collect the milk, he thought. But the rapping was repeated again and again.

'Mr. Leopard,' whispered Brer Anansi, 'the delivery is here. Mr. Leopard?'

But there was no answer. Quickly Brer Anansi lit his lamp and quietly searched the whole house. There was no Mr. Leopard to be seen. The rapping came again and Mr. Thunder roared, 'Brer Anansi, open this door or I will break it down!'

Of course, Brer Anansi was not so stupid as to open the door and get himself killed. He silently opened his back door and slid down his silk rope that led to the ground below. He was safe as long as Mr. Thunder did not get his hands on him.

Since then, Brer Anansi always ran to hide in a dark hole when he heard Mr. Thunder roaring in the skies. He also remembered that the same trick cannot work thrice!

The Fishing Trip

Brer Anansi wanted to go fishing but he had no hooks. The shops hadn't any. Brer Rabbit and Brer Bear had bought the last of the hooks and were determined to fish the river dry! It was no use Brer Anansi asking either of them for some hooks, they were sure to chase him away.

Since I cannot get the hooks, said Brer Anansi, I will get the fishes! He went under the jetty in his small rowing boat and waited at the end of it, keeping well out of sight. He could see Brer Bear's and Brer Rabbit's lines dangling down into the calm waters of the river.

Ten minutes later, Brer Rabbit felt a tug on his line. When he pulled it up he found he had caught an old boot. His line twitched again a few minutes later. This time he caught a bottle. He just couldn't understand it!

'Brer Bear,' he said, 'something tugged my line twice. I caught only an old boot and a bottle. I can't understand it at all!'

'Just bad luck, pal,' said Brer Bear. Just then his line was tugged. When he pulled it up, he was astonished to see a stick fastened to his hook.

'Well, I'll be sure-footed!' exclaimed Brer Bear. 'Just what is going on? We have caught nothing but rubbish!'

Indeed, they had been catching fish. But as soon as they had a bite, Brer Anansi quickly took the fish for himself and fastened one of the objects he had in his boat to the hook. He had kept well under the jetty so that his two enemies were unaware of his presence.

'I would say that Brer Anansi is responsible for this,' said Brer Bear. 'But he cannot swim or dive so he can't be down in the water.'

'Of course not!' exclaimed Brer Rabbit. 'He can't be in the water! Besides we bought all the hooks so he must be at home sleeping.'

The two friends rebaited their hooks and threw them down into the water. Some time later both hooks gave a sharp tug and the two friends quickly pulled them in. What a surprise they got. One fish was caught by both Brer Rabbit's and Brer Bear's hooks.

How should they divide it?

'This place is getting weirder,' said Brer Rabbit. 'I think that this place is spooked.'

'I am beginning to think so too,' added Brer Bear.

Meanwhile, Brer Anansi was counting his catch. He already had five fish. The fishing was good for him, very good. He was so keen on examining his fish that he didn't see Brer Rabbit looking down at him!

Brer Rabbit whispered to Brer Bear, 'I know what's wrong now! Brer Anansi is down below in a boat and he is taking all our fish. Let's teach him a lesson.'

'How?' asked Brer Bear.

'We will wait until the tide goes out a little more. The current will pull the boat out. Then we will take away the oars, seize our fish and cast him adrift!'

The tide ran down quickly and Brer Anansi did not realize that his boat could be seen at the end of the jetty. Brer Rabbit quickly grabbed the bow and pulled the boat out into the open water. Brer Bear grabbed the oars and fish, and Brer Rabbit pushed the boat out into the water.

'Now, fish-stealer, let's see how you will get out of this one. The boat will drift out into the ocean and you will never see the land again!'

'Oh, yes,' added Brer Rabbit. 'Good riddance to bad rubbish, I say. Happy fishing, Brer Anansi!'

'Please, Brer Rabbit! Please, let me have one oar back or I will drown!'

'You are getting no oar back! Serves you right for stealing our fish!'

The current took the boat out into the middle of the river. Brer Anansi was afraid. He could hardly see the banks of the river. The river was very wide! What should he do?

He stood helplessly and looked about. He could do nothing! He sat down in the bottom of the boat and started to cry. Big tears rolled down his black face. Then he heard a thump along the sides of the boat and saw Brer Alligator raising his head from the muddy waters of the river.

'Well, well, if it isn't Brer Anansi! What are you doing here all alone, pal?'

Brer Anansi and Brer Alligator were not friends, just ordinary pals. They did not like each other but they did not fight all the time.

'Oh,' replied Brer Anansi, quickly drying his tears, 'I am going on a cruise in this big wide river!'

'Is that so?' asked Brer Alligator. 'But you are sure going to be surprised. The current is taking you out into the big wide ocean!'

'That is grand! Just grand! What a cruise this is going to be!' exclaimed Brer Anansi. 'It is an honour to be pulled by this strong, majestic river and taken into the wide, wide ocean!'

'What do you mean by saying that this river is strong?' asked Brer Alligator, getting very angry. 'I am stronger than the current!'

'Eh? Is that so? You stronger than the current?' Brer Anansi laughed aloud.

'What is so funny, pal?' asked Brer Alligator.

'You are, Brer Alligator. Saying that you are stronger than the current! Why, the current is stronger because it takes this boat to the ocean!'

'Is that so? Throw down that tow-rope and I will take the boat to the shore. I, Brer Alligator, King of the River, Stronger Than the Current, will battle the current!'

Brer Alligator caught the tow-rope that Brer Anansi threw down to him and began pulling the boat to the shore. Inch by inch the boat crawled nearer the shore. Brer Anansi's plan was working. In a few minutes he was safe on the banks of the river. He tied the boat to a tree and turned to Brer Alligator.

'Yes, you are strong, Brer Alligator, stronger than I

thought. By the way, if I am permitted to ask, what makes you so strong?'

Brer Anansi looked down at the smiling Brer Alligator who puffed out his chest and said, 'Well, you see, I eat plenty of fish. I eat dozens and dozens of fish every day!'

'How do you get all that fish, Brer Alligator?' Brer Anansi was up to another of his tricks.

'I just swim below and gobble up most of the fish.'

'I bet you can't fill this boat with fish.'

'Can't I?' said Brer Alligator. He dived down into the muddy water. Brer Anansi waited. A minute later a hundred fishes jumped out of the water and into Brer Anansi's boat!

When Brer Alligator surfaced and saw the boat full of fish, he smiled. 'See, I just dive under and frighten the fish out of the water. Now are you satisfied that I am stronger than the current and a good catcher of fish?'

'Yes, yes, but there is another thing.'

'Oh, what is that?' asked Brer Alligator.

'I am wondering if you are strong enough to pull this boat of fishes and me to the jetty?'

Brer Alligator did not argue. He grabbed the rope from Brer Anansi and began pulling the boat towards the jetty which was a mile away. The current was strong but Brer Alligator was stronger. He was a powerful swimmer and they soon came in sight of the jetty. There was no sign of Brer Bear or Brer Rabbit.

After tying up the boat, Brer Anansi turned to Brer Alligator, 'Now I know that you really are stronger than the current, and a very powerful swimmer too. There can't be another water animal as strong as you.'

'Why, thank you, Brer Anansi,' said Brer Alligator. 'I am glad you admit that I am stronger than the current. And

King of the River too. Now I have to go. 'Bye for now!'

Brer Alligator disappeared under the muddy waters of the river. Just then the weasel came running down the jetty.

'Brer Anansi, I want to buy the fish that you have there. How much for the lot?'

'Oh, I would say about a barrow of tinned peaches!'

'Agreed!' said the weasel, and ran back to his shop. He came back with a barrow of tinned peaches, handed it to Brer Anansi, and set about unloading the fish. He had all hundred piled up on the jetty when Brer Bear and Brer Rabbit came running up.

'Where did you get those fish, Brer Anansi?' asked Brer Bear.

'Oh, down by the creek. There are plenty there. It's a pity that the boat is so small. I am going back there, though, for another load.'

'Oh, no you don't!' said Brer Rabbit, and he and Brer Bear leapt into the boat and pushed off. They were about ten yards from the jetty when Brer Bear shouted, 'Hey! Where are the oars?'

'The current is taking us out!' cried Brer Rabbit, in fright.

The two friends jumped out of the boat and swam towards the jetty. Meanwhile, Brer Anansi made for home with his barrow of tinned peaches before his two enemies could reach firm ground!

The Fancy Dress Party

'Brer Anansi! Brer Anansi!'

Brer Anansi was fast asleep. He did not hear Brer Monkey call him.

'BRER ANANSI! You lazy Brer Anansi, WAKE UP!'

Brer Anansi jumped out of bed. At last he was awake, but very angry. He had been having such a wonderful dream when Brer Monkey woke him up.

'Brer Monkey!' shouted Brer Anansi from his window. 'What do you mean by waking me up so early? It is only nine o'clock in the morning and I was having such a wonderful dream. I dreamt that I was King of Plantain Land and was surrounded by bunches and bunches and bunches of plantains. Fat, nice, ripe plantains. You had to come along and spoil it all!'

Brer Monkey leapt on to the window sill from the branch of an overhanging tree. He handed Brer Anansi a small, white envelope.

'Here, King Leo is having a party at three this afternoon and you are hereby invited. A prize will be given to the animal who has the most unusual costume.'

Brer Monkey leapt onto the branch again and was off among the trees to deliver the other letters the King had given him. Thinking about the contest, Brer Anansi went back to bed.

'Let me see,' he muttered to himself. 'I will certainly need a really fancy costume. Brer Bear and Brer Rabbit are sure to arrive in something outlandish, so I have to think of a weirder one. But what?'

Brer Anansi thought and thought but he could not think of any strange costume. It was not until he was preparing his breakfast that he had an idea. He would make a suit of armour, like the ones that the knights used when they went to battle.

After breakfast he went to the scrap heap. There he found plenty of iron things he could use to make his costume. There was a pot for his head, iron tins he would fix on his arms and legs by cutting out the bottoms, an old iron tub to go around his body and two old baking tins he could use for shoes.

Brer Anansi assembled his costume by using pieces of cloth and strong glue to make the joints. He spent most of the morning joining the parts together. Just after midday

38

his costume was ready. He took it for a trial run.

It fitted him well, but there was one fault. It was just a bit too heavy. But Brer Anansi did not mind this.

'I'll take it in my wheelbarrow and hide it in some bushes near the empty cornfield where the party is to be held. When three o'clock comes I will only have to walk a few yards wearing it.'

He took the costume towards the field. So far so good, thought Brer Anansi, no one has seen me. My costume is really going to be a surprise. I am sure to win. But he was seen by Brer Rabbit and Brer Bear. The two friends were working on their costume when Brer Rabbit heard the wheelbarrow coming along the road. The two of them hid behind some bushes and saw Brer Anansi deposit his costume in a thick clump of hedges. They waited until he had left, then went to inspect the armour.

'It's good,' said Brer Rabbit. 'Brer Anansi stands a good chance of winning.'

'That is if he turns out in it,' added Brer Bear.

'What do you mean?' Brer Rabbit asked.

'We will hide the costume,' explained the crafty Brer Bear, 'so he will have no costume to wear. Then we'll be sure to win!'

Brer Rabbit smiled. 'A wonderful idea!'

Meanwhile, Brer Anansi was having a bath. He hardly ever bathed but this was an exception. He knew that it would be a very hot afternoon, and he would get even hotter inside the metal costume. He decided to wear the costume with only a small sheet tied around his waist as he would be more comfortable without any clothes.

By half past two Brer Anansi was all ready to go. With a sheet tied around his waist he started off towards the clump of bushes where he had left his wheelbarrow and metal costume. And what a shock he got when he peered into the bushes. Only an empty barrow met his gaze!

'I know,' said Brer Anansi. 'Brer Rabbit and Brer Bear must have hidden my costume. I will go and see them about this!'

First he went to Brer Bear's house. The gate was locked. Brer Bear was not at home. He hurried to Brer Rabbit's burrow. It was getting late. Brer Anansi had to find his costume soon or else he would be too late for the party.

He found the two friends trying on their costume—a donkey's skin. It was in two halves. Brer Rabbit was just stepping inside the front half. Brer Bear was already in his back half. Brer Anansi stopped and looked on.

'Come on, Brer Rabbit,' said Brer Bear. 'Hurry up or we will be late.'

'I know, I know. I am doing the best I can,' explained Brer Rabbit. 'I know what we will do. We will take the short cut across Farmer Brown's carrot field.'

Brer Anansi had an idea. He knew how he would catch the two friends at their own game. He hurried off to tell Farmer Brown about the 'donkey' in his carrot field.

Ten minutes later a donkey walked quietly into Farmer Brown's carrot field. It was a very strange donkey, indeed. The head was much lower than the back because Brer Rabbit was in front and Brer Bear was at the back.

Farmer Brown waited silently at the other end of the field. He had a big stick in his hands. I will teach those two rascals a lesson, thought Farmer Brown, dressing up like a donkey just to steal my carrots.

The donkey was now in the centre of the field. Only Brer Rabbit, who was in the head-part of the donkey, could see. Brer Bear had to follow blindly.

'Are we there yet?' asked Brer Bear.

'No, stupid! We are only in Farmer Brown's field. What nice, juicy carrots he has here!'

'Never mind the carrots, Brer Rabbit,' said Brer Bear. 'Just keep going or we will be late for the party.'

'O.K., O.K., Brer Bear! No pushing, I am going as fast as I can!'

The donkey was nearly across the field. Brer Rabbit did not see Farmer Brown creep up from behind.

Whap! Farmer Brown landed a good blow on Brer Bear's rear. The blow was so sudden that Brer Bear jumped forward, colliding with Brer Rabbit. The donkey fell over in a heap!

'Why are you pushing, Brer Bear?' asked Brer Rabbit. 'Can't you see that I am going as fast as I can?'

'I didn't push you,' said Brer Bear, picking himself up. 'I was kicked from behind.'

'Kicked from behind! How can a donkey kick itself from behind? Just stop telling tales and keep walking.'

The donkey continued across the field as before. Farmer Brown waited a while and then whap! Brer Bear got another blow from the huge stick!

'Yeow!' He yelled, again colliding with Brer Rabbit.

'What is the matter, Brer Bear? Can't you stop pushing? If you push again, I will—Ouch!'

This time it was Brer Rabbit who got the blow. Brer Bear was pleased that Brer Rabbit was now aware that it was not he who had been doing all the pushing.

'Are you satisfied now, Brer Rabbit?' asked Brer Bear. 'It was not I who is pushing but—YEOW!'

Brer Bear got the next blow and Brer Rabbit got the other one. Soon the donkey was a fighting, pushing and tumbling mass. Brer Rabbit was trying to go one way while Brer Bear was pulling the other way. They couldn't go in opposite directions because neither of them remembered the zip that held the halves of the costume together. Farmer Brown continued hitting them until he was tired. How his hands ached!

The two friends struggled harder than ever. They were both in pain and eager to be off. But they couldn't get anywhere for they pulled in different directions. At last the costume came apart. Both friends were off in a flash. Brer Rabbit got away, and Farmer Brown chased Brer Bear who was struggling hard to get out of the costume.

How Brer Anansi laughed and laughed! He was waiting outside the field in his sheet. He roared with laughter when the costume ripped in two and his two enemies ran off in separate directions.

Brer Anansi went homewards because he hadn't found his costume to go to the party. He was so happy that tears of laughter streamed down his face. Blinded by tears he failed to realize that he was heading straight for the corn-field.

He was already in the cornfield when he was suddenly aware of the other animals. Wiping his eyes, he looked around. There were all sorts of costumes. The hare wore a spotted pyjama suit, the squirrel a sort of bathing costume, and the monkey had on a white shirt and a bow-tie. Brer Anansi was ashamed. All the animals surrounded him and were laughing at what they thought was his costume.

'Ho there, Brer Anansi,' said squirrel. 'You have forgotten your nursing bottle at home!'

'Where is your mother, sonny boy!' called the monkey.

'It is long past your bedtime, boy,' added the snail.

Brer Anansi was ashamed. Every animal present had mistaken the sheet for a nappy. He was just like a baby now! He was beginning to feel sorry he had ever thought of a metal costume when the King spoke.

'Brer Anansi has the most unusual costume, without a doubt. He has won the prize as far as I can see. Does anyone disagree?'

'Of course not, sire,' said most of the animals. 'We all agree that he should collect his prize.'

And Brer Anansi marched proudly up to the King for his barrow full of tinned peaches!

Brer Anansi's Bravery

Brer Anansi was tired of walking to and from market so he decided to buy a donkey. At first he tied the donkey under his house, but after two weeks, the donkey was used to his new surroundings and Brer Anansi allowed him to roam about untied.

Late one afternoon, Brer Anansi was entertaining his guest, Brer Weasel. They were relaxing after tea and Brer Weasel was relating his experiences to his host.

'I remember once,' he said, 'how I created a lot of

excitement in the village. I turned up there one day with an egg in a small-necked bottle. You can guess how surprised the villagers were. Even Brer Bear and Brer Rabbit were surprised to see the egg in the bottle and they bought a dozen eggs just to put one in a bottle. But they didn't know that the egg has to be soaked in vinegar for two weeks so that it will become soft like foam.'

Brer Anansi laughed. 'Yes, I too have been having a lot of trouble from Brer Bear and Brer Rabbit. I am willing to bet that they are afraid of me, really. But they don't know that I am afraid of Tip-Tip-Wah.'

While they were talking, a ferocious tiger who had stolen from King Leo had crept under Brer Anansi's tree-house to spend the night. He heard all that Brer Anansi said and wondered about this Tip-Tip-Wah. Who could it be? He reasoned that since Brer Anansi was afraid of him and Brer Anansi was not afraid of Brer Bear or Brer Rabbit, then Tip-Tip-Wah must really be somebody brave and strong. I will remember to keep well clear of this Tip-Tip-Wah, thought tiger.

Just then Mr. Thunder roared up above and began shaking the clouds about. Brer Anansi looked out of his window and shook his head.

'You know, Brer Weasel, Tip-Tip-Wah will be coming anytime now. I smell him just around the corner. I had better go and tie my donkey under the house for the night. I don't want him to get wet.'

Tiger was not awake to hear that Brer Anansi was coming down to tie up his donkey. Indeed, he was fast asleep and snoring his head off. Brer Anansi slid down his silk rope but it was so dark that he misjudged where the ground was and fell down with a sharp thud. He picked himself up and looked around. It was so dark that he could hardly see more than three feet in front of him. Tiger heard the thud when Brer Anansi landed, and he remained still. What was that he had heard Brer Anansi say about Tip-Tip-Wah coming?

Tiger was afraid. He crouched down low and waited. Brer Anansi, meanwhile, stretched out his hands and groped about for his donkey. He had to hurry. Mr. Thunder was roaring up above and soon Tip-Tip-Wah would come!

He tripped against tiger's tail, and thinking it was his donkey's, he grabbed hold of it and tied a piece of rope around tiger's neck. Tiger remained still. He did not resist at all, for he thought that it was Tip-Tip-Wah who was tying him up. Brer Anansi tied the free end of the rope to a stump and climbed up into his house.

The rain came down soon after and it continued all night. Brer Weasel had to spend the night with Brer Anansi. Early next morning, just as the rain was over, he looked down and the first thing he saw was the tiger tied to a stump.

'Brer Anansi! Brer Anansi! Come and look at this! Come quickly!'

Brer Anansi jumped out of bed and looked down at the tiger. 'How did he get here?' asked Brer Anansi.

'Remember about the donkey that you tied up last night? Well, it appears that you made a mistake. That tiger down there is wanted by King Leo. I will go and tell the King. You will be well rewarded!'

Brer Anansi trembled. He thought of how tiger could have bitten him when he tied him up. Why didn't tiger bite him? Brer Anansi could not think of a reason.

Brer Weasel soon returned with a small bag of gold coins. He handed this to Brer Anansi and they both watched as the Court Gorilla carried tiger away. Soon all the animals knew how brave Brer Anansi was! Tiger did not know that

Tip-Tip-Wah was the name by which Brer Anansi called the rain. No animal ever knew the truth about the tiger that Brer Anansi had captured.

But that was not the end of the matter. Oh no! Brer Bear and Brer Rabbit were the only ones who did not believe that Brer Anansi was all that brave.

'He is nothing but a pretender and a rogue!' said Brer Rabbit, getting red about the ears.

'I agree with you. Someone has to teach that loud-mouth a good lesson!' grumbled Brer Bear.

'I know what,' said Brer Rabbit, 'let US teach him a lesson. I know of a way—it's sure to work! Listen carefully.'

Brer Rabbit spoke rapidly to Brer Bear for two minutes. Then they went into Brer Rabbit's burrow and remained there for some time.

Half an hour later Brer Anansi was surprised to see Brer Bear looking up at him.

'Brer Anansi,' he said, 'I am challenging you to a test of bravery. You are to come to the old house at seven this evening and we will see who is braver. If you don't turn up I will tell all the animals what a coward you are!'

Brer Anansi shouted back at Brer Bear. 'Yes, I'll be there! The great Brer Anansi will be there!'

But Brer Bear only smiled and said softly, 'You will be running for your life, you coward. You just wait and see!'

Brer Anansi was no fool. He left for the old house an hour before the appointed time. He wanted to inspect the various traps that his enemy must have prepared for him.

The house was all still and silent. Brer Anansi walked up the creaking stair and opened the door. Cobwebs hung everywhere. He brushed them away and went into the only bedroom he could see. Just inside the room there were two white sheets on the floor. So, Brer Rabbit and Brer Bear are up to their old tricks again, thought Brer Anansi. But this time I will be ready for them. Dressing up as ghosts!

Seven o'clock saw Brer Bear and Brer Rabbit near to the house. Brer Rabbit waited outside to warn Brer Bear when Brer Anansi was coming. Brer Bear was all excited. He ran into the house and straight into the bedroom. As soon as he opened the door a sack of flour fell on him. The paper sacking broke and he was white all over. He didn't mind this at all. He didn't even wonder how the flour got there. He just threw one of the sheets over his head and peered through the holes he had cut for his eyes. Now he would wait for Brer Anansi to come along.

Brer Bear soon grew impatient and began to walk about on the creaking floorboards. He didn't look where he was going and stepped on the end of a loose board. The other end sprang up sharply and gave him a good whack on the forehead. He was knocked out cold!

'All the better,' said Brer Anansi from inside the cupboard. 'It saves me the bother of knocking him out myself.'

Half an hour later Brer Rabbit came into the house. He was angry, very angry.

'You know, Brer Bear, that coward—' He stopped short when he saw the still form of his friend on the floor. 'Brer Bear? What's wrong?'

He shook Brer Bear but got no answer. 'He is dead, struck on the head by a ghost!'

He didn't see the flour, for Brer Bear was still wearing the sheet, and besides, it was somewhat dark inside the house. 'I'm getting out of here,' he said, and ran for the door. In his haste he failed to notice the string that was tied across the doorway and held taut by Brer Anansi from a hole in the cupboard. He fell from the top of the stairs right down to the bottom. He lay panting on the moonlit ground.

Meanwhile Brer Bear woke up. He got to his feet and grumbled to himself.

'That floorboard! Brer Anansi is the cause of all this confusion. I am going to see Brer Rabbit about this.'

He threw off the sheet and marched towards the door. He stopped just before the twine across the doorway when he saw Brer Rabbit flat on the ground outside. At the same time Brer Rabbit looked up and saw the white form of Brer Bear in the moonlight. How white he was!

Suddenly Brer Rabbit remembered that Brer Bear was supposed to be dead. He scrambled to his feet and backed away.

'No, no, keep away! Brer Bear stay away. It's me, your friend, Brer Rabbit!'

'What is he on about?' grumbled Brer Bear. 'He must be going crackers or something. It must be the moonlight.'

'Whooo!' Brer Bear heard the noise coming from just behind and turned round. A shape in a white sheet was coming slowly up to him.

'Brer Rabbit,' asked Brer Bear, 'where is Brer Anansi— Brer Rabbit!'

At first he thought that the person in the white sheet was Brer Rabbit, then he remembered that Brer Rabbit was down below. Then he didn't stay to ask who it was. He just made a dash for the ground below, failed to see the string, and was sent flying down.

Brer Rabbit saw the white Brer Bear leap into the air and thought that it was the flying ghost of his friend coming to get him. He turned and ran down the road as fast as he could. Brer Bear landed with a sharp thump on the hard earth, leapt to his feet and ran after Brer Rabbit.

Brer Rabbit looked back and saw his friend coming behind, and thinking that he was after him, he gathered

49

more speed. Brer Bear thought that Brer Rabbit was running away from the ghost that was chasing him and he didn't bother to look back. Brer Anansi had stopped chasing Brer Bear long ago. He had taken a short cut so that he came out directly in front of Brer Rabbit.

What a shock Brer Rabbit got! He saw a ghost coming up in front of him, and when he looked back he saw the white Brer Bear still coming after him. I will chance it, thought Brer Rabbit hastily. Since I cannot run off the road because of the thick woods along the sides, I will see if my old friend will help me. So he stopped and ran straight for Brer Bear!

Brer Bear was surprised. Why is Brer Rabbit running this way now? It means that the ghost has flown over both of us and is after him now. He saw the white sheet coming up after Brer Rabbit and he too turned and ran in the opposite direction. Brer Anansi in a white sheet was chasing Brer Rabbit who was chasing after Brer Bear. Brer Bear was running away from the white sheet.

All three of them ran past the old house and down the road as fast as they could. Brer Bear was perspiring. His sweat mixed with the flour and he felt sticky all over. Brer Rabbit was rapidly becoming tired. He realized that he was trapped between two ghosts.

Brer Rabbit scratched his head as he ran. Something is funny about all this, he thought. Why should the ghost of Brer Bear run away from another ghost? Unless Brer Bear was not a ghost himself.

The moon disappeared behind a cloud, and just as darkness descended, Brer Rabbit ducked behind some bushes by the side of the road and waited.

When the moon peered out from behind the cloud a minute later, Brer Anansi was surprised to see no sign of

Brer Rabbit. Brer Bear looked back too, and seeing no sign of Brer Rabbit, he reasoned that the ghost must have got him already. He quickened his pace. Brer Rabbit waited until the ghost had passed his hiding place, and followed after.

Brer Rabbit was now after Brer Anansi, who was after Brer Bear. Brer Anansi was most surprised. Where was Brer Rabbit? He had been in the middle and now there was no sign of him at all. On an impulse, he looked back and saw him coming behind. Now Brer Anansi was trapped by his two enemies!

'Brer Bear, Brer Bear!' shouted Brer Rabbit.'Turn back! The ghost is Brer Anansi in a white sheet!'

His guess had been correct, for the ghost in the white sheet stopped abruptly. Brer Bear turned back and saw the ghost in the white sheet stop. He advanced upon Brer Anansi, who was becoming afraid. They had seen through his trick!

He stood silently and waited. There was no use making a dash for it. He was trapped; his two enemies were advancing upon him. There was one way out, but he had to be quick about it. All he had to do was throw the sheet over the flour-strewn Brer Bear and make a dash for it. It might just work!

Brer Anansi waited until Brer Bear came close, then quickly took off the sheet, threw it over the sticky Brer Bear, and made a dash for it. Brer Bear struggled to free himself.

Brer Anansi was now on the run. Brer Rabbit came after him, followed by Brer Bear, who was using the sheet to wipe the flour from his fur as he ran.

The spider was sorry that he ever mentioned to Brer Weasel that he was afraid of Tip-Tip-Wah, the rain. Now he would suffer if his two enemies caught up with him. 'Me and my big mouth,'grumbled Brer Anansi as he ran.

Of course, he managed to escape by reaching home before they could catch him!

The Lucky Escape

'Fire? How?' asked Brer Bear.

'Simple!' said Brer Rabbit. 'We will wait until he is asleep and then set fire to his house. In that way we will get rid of Brer Anansi!'

'Bravo! Excellent!' exclaimed Brer Bear.

'Right,' said Brer Rabbit, 'let's get over there right now. He must be asleep.'

The two crept out into the night and went directly to Brer Anansi's tree-house. They heaped dry branches under the trunk of the tree and Brer Bear struck a match. Soon the tree was on fire. It burned a bright red and sparks flew everywhere.

In an hour, the tree-house was a black stump sticking out into the ground!

The two friends went home well satisfied that they had got rid of their enemy, Brer Anansi, for good.

The next morning Brer Rabbit and Brer Bear went to the market very early. They brought back two barrows full of vegetables and canned food and set up all the pots they had. They invited all the animals for lunch. They were going to celebrate the death of Brer Anansi.

An hour before lunch all the animals were assembled in a clearing in the forest. Brer Rabbit was in charge of the pots of food and Brer Bear was seated in the centre. He was reading from a little black book. In it was written all the foul deeds that Brer Anansi had done to the two friends.

While the reading was going on, who should happen to come along but Brer Anansi! He had not been in his house as Brer Rabbit and Brer Bear thought, but had spent the night at Brer Weasel's house. Early in the morning Brer Anansi went home but he could not see any signs of his house. Only a black stump remained, so, thinking that Mr. Thunder must have burnt down his house during the night, he went to cut new posts to rebuild it. Now he was coming back with a post over his shoulders.

The animals there saw him coming and they were very surprised. Brer Anansi was supposed to be dead, yet he was coming up the path with a post. They became afraid and crept away, one by one, very quietly.

Only Brer Bear and Brer Rabbit were left. Brer Rabbit was too busy over his pots to notice what was happening and Brer Bear was too busy reading to notice either.

Brer Rabbit suddenly looked up and got a shock. As soon as he saw Brer Anansi with the post, he took to his heels, leaving the pots of food on the ground. Brer Anansi came up and leaned against his post as if it were a walking stick. He watched the busy Brer Bear.

His head was down over his book and he was lost to the world. Then suddenly he looked up as he turned a page, and stared wide-eyed at Brer Anansi. He remained there for a few seconds and then sprang up. He ran to Brer Anansi's donkey which was tied to a stump, and sprang on. Without even untying the rope from the stump, he whipped the donkey forward. The donkey gave a sharp tug and the peg flew out of the ground.

In two seconds he was down the path as fast as the donkey could go. Brer Bear was very much afraid, for Brer Anansi was supposed to be dead and now there he was, looking down at Brer Bear with a post at the ready. Brer Bear thought that Brer Anansi was about to beat him with the post!

Now what is going on here, wondered Brer Anansi, looking around. He just couldn't understand it. First, all the animals ran away when they saw him coming, then Brer Rabbit ran away when he saw him, and finally, Brer Bear ran for his life when he noticed Brer Anansi with the post. Brer Anansi stood and scratched his head in wonder.

Meanwhile, Brer Bear was well down the path on Brer Anansi's donkey. The rope dangled behind and the two-foot peg bounced in the air, and knocked Brer Bear hard on the head.

Brer Bear felt the blow on his head and thought that his enemy, Brer Anansi, who was supposed to be dead, was chasing after him and was hitting him on the head with a post. He beat his donkey harder and harder and the stump sprang up again and again and knocked him on the head.

The donkey was becoming tired. It sank to its knees and Brer Bear was sent flying over its head. He landed on some stones and remained still.

Brer Rabbit, by this time, was dashing through the bushes as fast as he could go. He, too, just couldn't understand it. What was Brer Anansi doing with the post when he was supposed to be dead? Brer Rabbit ran and ran and ran. He met Brer Bear who had recovered himself, and both of them ran out of the forest. They stopped a few miles away and decided not to return for some weeks.

What about Brer Anansi? Oh, he just started eating all the food lying about in the pots. He just couldn't understand what really had happened, but he didn't care. He was hungry, very hungry, and there was plenty of food about!

The Rainbow's End

One bright April morning Brer Anansi saw the most beautiful rainbow in the world. At least *he* thought that it was the most beautiful rainbow in the world. It had all the possible colours he could think of—blue, red, green, yellow and many others. The rainbow was simply beautiful.

Brer Anansi scratched his head and looked again at the rainbow. 'Now I seem to remember some tale,' he said to himself, 'that rainbows have a pot of gold at one end.' It might be true, he decided, so I will go and look for it. But first I have to prepare a meal as it might be a very long journey.

After Brer Anansi had tied up a meal in a handkerchief and tied it to the end of a stick, he set off on his search for the pot of gold. He had hardly covered half a mile when he met Brer Buzzard.

'Where are you off to, Brer Anansi?' asked Brer Buzzard.

'I am off to the end of the rainbow,' replied Brer Anansi, looking up at the big, beautiful rainbow.

'To the end of the rainbow?' repeated Brer Buzzard. 'But that is a very long journey. I have often tried flying there but there seems to be no end to that colourful band in the skies. What are you going there for, by the way?'

Brer Anansi was not stupid. He knew that if he told Brer Buzzard, the bird would follow him; he could fly faster and might reach the end of the rainbow first and collect all the gold.

'Oh,' replied Brer Anansi carelessly, 'I feel like taking a long walk today so I have decided to follow the rainbow. Care to come along?'

'Oh, no! Not me!' replied Brer Buzzard, shaking his head. 'I would never get there even if I fly for a year.'

Brer Anansi was left to continue his journey alone. All the better, for he wanted the gold for himself. Brer Buzzard was flying homewards when he saw Brer Bear taking his morning stroll. He flew down, keeping well out of reach, and said:

'You know what, Brer Bear? Brer Anansi is on his way to the end of the rainbow. He says he needs a lot of exercise today.'

'Who cares where he is going to?' replied Brer Bear. 'If he wants to go to the end of the rainbow, let him go!'

After Brer Buzzard had flown away, Brer Bear scratched

his head.' I seem to remember,' he said,' some story about the rainbow. Wait, I remember now! There is a pot of gold at the end. So that's what Brer Anansi is after, but not if I can help it!' Brer Bear followed quickly after Brer Anansi. He too wanted the gold.

Meanwhile, Brer Buzzard met Brer Rabbit. He kept well out of Brer Rabbit's reach because he knew that if Brer Rabbit got hold of him he would pull out all his feathers, one by one, by way of repaying all the ill deeds that he had done to Brer Rabbit in the past.

'Brer Rabbit, Brer Anansi is off to the end of the rainbow, and so is Brer Bear.'

Brer Rabbit picked up a stone and threw it at Brer Buzzard. 'Off with you! I don't need you around. Mischief maker!'

Brer Rabbit was smart. After Brer Buzzard had disappeared among the trees, he followed Brer Bear. He knew that since Brer Bear was following Brer Anansi, something was up, and he wanted to know what.

The three adventurers were off to the end of the rainbow. Brer Anansi was about two miles ahead of Brer Bear and Brer Rabbit took up the rear. They had been travelling for ten minutes when Brer Anansi became tired. He wanted to rest. The sun was rising higher in the sky and it was very hot. Brer Anansi climbed up a tree where the blowing leaves made him feel cooler. He soon became too comfortable to move and decided to stay up there awhile.

Brer Bear saw Brer Anansi go into the woods, still following the rainbow, so he followed after. But when he came to the woods, there was no sign of Brer Anansi at all.

'Where can he have gone to?' said Brer Bear, looking around. He sat under a tree and decided to rest a little and then go and look for Brer Anansi. Without knowing it he had sat under the same tree that Brer Anansi was in. Brer Anansi kept very still. He didn't want Brer Bear to know that he was up there as he might follow him when he resumed his journey. He did not know that Brer Bear had been following him for some time now.

Brer Rabbit, seeing Brer Bear go into the woods too, followed him in. He thought that Brer Bear would be walking after Brer Anansi but when he came to the clearing in the woods, he saw Brer Bear sitting under a tree.

Brer Bear got quite excited when he saw Brer Rabbit. 'What are you doing here?' asked Brer Bear.

'Oh, I saw you coming in here all stealthy-like so I decided to follow you,' replied Brer Rabbit.

'I was following Brer Anansi and he seems to have disappeared,' explained Brer Bear.

'I wonder where he could have gone to,' said Brer Rabbit. 'He could not have gone to the end of the rainbow without our seeing him.'

Brer Anansi stood perfectly still on a branch of the tree. So, his two enemies had followed him. The two wanted the gold for themselves, thought Brer Anansi. He listened to what the two were saying.

'I know what we should do,' said Brer Bear. 'You go and look for him over there and I will look over this side of the tree. Shout and call me if you find him, and I will do the same if I find him before you.'

So the two separated. Each went in opposite directions. Brer Anansi watched as they disappeared noisily into the bushes. Soon the sound grew further and further away. Finally, there was silence. Brer Anansi came down from his tree and ate his snack. He was soon finished and climbed up the tree again.

Half an hour later, Brer Rabbit and Brer Bear returned.

They were both tired out and hungry. Their hides were inflamed and bruised where the thorns had pricked them. Brer Bear had a big bump on his nose where a bee had stung him.

'If ever I get my hands on that Brer Anansi, he'll be sorry that he tried to go to the end of the rainbow!' said Brer Bear, rubbing the end of his nose. How it pained him!

Brer Rabbit too was very, very angry. He had been scratched and bitten by all sorts of insects. He had even encountered bugs when he crawled under a rotten tree trunk to see if Brer Anansi was under it. Bats flew at him when he entered a cave.

'Let's take a bath,' said Brer Bear. 'It may help to cure our pains. But I can assure you that Brer Anansi will never cure his when I'm finished with him!'

The two friends disappeared into the bushes and Brer Anansi slid down from the tree. He followed them and saw them take off their clothes and plunge into a pond. He crawled quietly up to their clothes, took them away and proceeded to run some itch-bushes on them.

'That will teach them not to follow me about,' he said. 'I would have had the pot of gold already if they had kept away from the tree when I wanted to come down. Nosey idiots!'

Then he took the clothes back to the side of the pond and ran home. He took a pot from his kitchen cupboard and filled it to the brim with stones.

He went back to the pond and looked down at the two animals thrashing about in the water.

'Oh, my poor feet! This is worse,' said Brer Rabbit, almost in tears. 'I am still in pain.'

'If I ever get my hands on Brer Anansi!' said Brer Bear, and smacked his fists together.

'Is that so?' asked Brer Anansi. 'What have I done to deserve such treatment, you rogues!'

As soon as the two friends saw Brer Anansi, they roared together:

'There he is! After him! Tar his black furry skin! Never mind the gold in the pot. Don't let him get away!'

Quickly they clambered out of the water and put on their clothes. They were in such a hurry that they failed to notice the green, itchy leaves on their clothes.

Meanwhile Brer Anansi was off like a shot! He ran as fast as he could with his pot of stones. The two friends ran quickly after him as soon as they got their clothes on. They were catching up with Brer Anansi who could not run very fast with his pot of stones. But he didn't have to worry.

Brer Rabbit was a few yards behind Brer Anansi when he felt very funny. Something was tickling him. Then he felt itchy all over and scratched away as fast as he could. How he itched!

Brer Bear was amazed. He was a few yards behind and saw his friend stop abruptly and scratch furiously. 'What is wrong with him?' said Brer Bear to himself. He soon found out, for he too began feeling itchy. How he itched. The two friends were scratching away as fast as they could!

Brer Anansi laughed and laughed. It was great fun to see his two enemies scratching away like mad.

'Serves you right, Brer Bear, for following me, and you too, Brer Rabbit. In future, mind your own business!'

Brer Anansi ran home when he thought the itching was beginning to wear off. He had to be far away when his two enemies recovered. 'I will go and look for the gold another time,' said Brer Anansi, 'if Brer Rabbit and Brer Bear ever let me alone.'

The Carrot Swindle

One bright Saturday morning Brer Rabbit was going to market to sell his carrots when the wheel of his barrow came off. Brer Rabbit was very angry. He had to get to market early or else Farmer Brown would catch him selling the stolen carrots. Brer Rabbit never owned anything. He always stole carrots to sell whenever he wanted money to buy anything. He was too lazy to work.

Brer Rabbit did not know what to do. He could not get to the market without mending his barrow first, and if he should leave it and go back home for a nut to repair it, someone was sure to come along and steal his carrots. What was he to do?

Just then Brer Anansi happened to come along. He too was going to the market. As soon as he saw what was the matter with the barrow, he laughed aloud.

'Ah, Brer Rabbit! Farmer Brown will surely catch you today if you don't mend that barrow and sell the carrots before he sees you with them.'

'My friend,' said Brer Rabbit, putting aside all the wrong deeds that Brer Anansi had done to him, 'I would like you to give me a hand with this barrow. Why don't you stay here and watch it for me until I return? I will give you ten carrots.'

Brer Anansi thought over the offer. It was tempting, but if Farmer Brown happened to come along and catch him with the carrots, then he would be in a terrible fix.

'I am sorry,' Brer Anansi told Brer Rabbit. 'I can't do that for you. It's too great a risk. Besides, ten carrots are too little.'

Brer Rabbit increased his offer to fifteen. He had about fifty carrots, they were all big and juicy and he could very well do away with fifteen. Anyway, they were not really his.

Brer Anansi agreed to accept the offer of fifteen carrots. Brer Rabbit smiled and ran down the road to his house. He knew that Brer Anansi could not take away his carrots because he could not carry them away before he returned. But he was mistaken. Brer Anansi had one of his plans!

Brer Anansi waited until Brer Rabbit was out of sight. He then started unloading the barrow. The carrots were too much for him to take home as he lived far away and he could only carry five at a time. He hid the carrots away in some nearby bushes where they were safe. Only he knew where they were. Now he would leave the barrow and wait up a tree for Brer Rabbit to return.

Brer Anansi had just hidden the carrots and was about to climb up a tall tree when Farmer Brown happened along. The farmer came up and pointed his gun at the barrow.

'Whose barrow is this?' he asked.

'Oh, it is Brer Rabbit's,' explained Brer Anansi. 'We were pushing each other about when the wheel came off. Brer Rabbit has gone home for a nut to fix it.'

'Hurumph!' said Farmer Brown. 'I was expecting to see it full of my carrots, but I am never lucky. I never catch Brer Rabbit with my carrots. I know he steals them, and one of these days, I will catch him!'

While Farmer Brown and Brer Anansi were talking, Brer Buzzard flew past. He saw the carrots in the bushes, and flew down to inspect them more closely. No one saw him.

Quietly he flew off with two carrots in his strong claws and took them some distance away where he hid them under some bushes. He returned for two more, another two, and yet another two. Soon he had thirty-four carrots hidden away. He was returning for another two when Farmer Brown strolled off. Brer Buzzard only managed to take one carrot this time. Only fifteen were left.

Brer Anansi did not bother to check to see if all his carrots were still there. He was more interested in getting away from Brer Rabbit. It is lucky for me, thought Brer Anansi, that I unloaded the barrow or Farmer Brown would have caught me with the carrots.

He was about to climb the tree again when Brer Rabbit came back. He had a nut with him. As soon as he saw the empty barrow, he grabbed hold of Brer Anansi who was struggling to climb up the tree.

'Where are my carrots?' demanded Brer Rabbit.

'Well, I saw Farmer Brown coming along so I hid them behind those bushes,' explained the terrified Brer Anansi.

'A likely story,' said Brer Rabbit. 'I don't believe it. All I know is that you have stolen my carrots and hidden them.'

'Why don't you check those bushes?' asked Brer Anansi.

'O.K., I will, just to satisfy you that there are no carrots there,' said Brer Rabbit, without even releasing Brer Anansi.

He went into the bushes dragging Brer Anansi along with him. Seeing the carrots in the bushes, he just took one look at the carrots and released Brer Anansi. Brer Rabbit bent down and picked up a few carrots. It was only then that he saw that there were only a few carrots there.

'Hey, Brer Anansi! There are only about fifteen carrots there. Where are the rest?'

Brer Anansi did not know what to make of it all. He had left fifty carrots there and now there was only fifteen. Someone must have stolen the rest.

Brer Anansi did not want to try and explain what must have happened. He quickly took to his heels down the road. Brer Rabbit hopped after him. 'The rascal,' said Brer Rabbit, 'stealing my carrots! I will teach him a lesson he will never forget.'

Now Brer Rabbit had galloped all the way from home with the nut and he was tired. He could not catch up with Brer Anansi. He panted and puffed behind Brer Anansi who was going quite fast. The spider was soon in his house. Brer Anansi pulled up the silk rope that led down to the ground.

Brer Rabbit waited down below. He had to make Brer Anansi pay for his crimes, but how? He could not climb up after him on the sticky webbing. He would be trapped there. Brer Anansi smiled down at him.

Brer Rabbit thought and thought of a plan. He wanted to

get back his carrots! Finally he found a solution to his problems. Pretending to be hungry, he went off in the direction of his house. When he was out of Brer Anansi's sight, he changed direction. He went to see Pete, the centipede. He borrowed a dozen pairs of old shoes and went back to where he had left Brer Anansi.

The spider was very surprised to see him again. He was puzzled. What is Brer Rabbit going to do with all those shoes, wondered Brer Anansi.

Brer Rabbit called up to Brer Anansi:

'Ho there, carrot stealer! I will catch you now. These are Pete's shoes. He has a good number of feet, you know, so he has plenty of old shoes. I have borrowed twenty-four and I will catch you now. Just you wait and see.'

Brer Anansi peered through the crack in his door. He saw Brer Rabbit place one big shoe in the sticky webbing and then he placed another in front to fit. Stepping neatly into the first shoe, he placed his foot in the other. He had all the other shoes in his hands and was going to line them up so he could reach Brer Anansi's door.

Brer Anansi was terrified. He realized that he was going to fall into Brer Rabbit's hands. He was going to pay for a crime that he did not commit. Of course, he had saved Brer Rabbit from Farmer Brown, but who would believe him?

Just then Farmer Brown ran up. 'Brer Rabbit! Brer Rabbit! I have to apologise to you.'

Farmer Brown had a barrow full of carrots with him. 'Here, take this, my friend. It appears that I was wrong about you stealing my carrots. I was waiting at the market to see if you would turn up with them, and I caught Brer Buzzard selling them. I apologise to you.'

Brer Rabbit collected the carrots and old shoes he had borrowed, and placed them in the barrow. After Farmer

Brown left, Brer Rabbit took out fifteen carrots from his barrow.

'Here, Brer Anansi, you really are a friend. I am sorry to have suspected you. I thank you for shifting the blame on to Brer Buzzard. I can bet he hasn't got any feathers left on his body now. Serves him right for taking the carrots. Now I can steal more from Farmer Brown and Brer Buzzard will get the blame from now. Once a thief always a thief, I say. So long, friend.'

Brer Rabbit wheeled his barrow homewards. After he had gone, Brer Anansi collected the fifteen carrots in his barrow. He was going to sell the carrots. On the road, he stopped by a familiar tree and took out the fifteen carrots that were left in the bushes nearby. He now had thirty to sell. Brer Rabbit had more, but he would always be suspected of stealing them. Everyone knows he steals, thought Brer Anansi.

His plan had worked after all!

The Catapult

'Look what I've found!' said Brer Anansi, with a big smile on his round, black face.

He bent down and picked up a catapult. He stretched the rubber about and smiled again. This catapult is good, he thought, I will go and have some fun. He went down to the stream and filled his pockets with round pebbles. Then he climbed up a tree and waited. He was waiting for Brer Bear and Brer Rabbit to come along.

Brer Rabbit came along first and stopped right under the tree. He didn't notice Brer Anansi up in the branches. He walked past for a few yards, then bent down to pick up a branch.

Smack! Something hit his rear with such force that he toppled over on his head. Some minutes later he got to his feet and rubbed his rear. What's going on around here, he wondered. After he felt satisfied that there was no one around, he bent down to pick up the branch again.

Smack! He felt a sharp pain in his rear again. Brer Rabbit rubbed hard and looked around. There was no one around as far as he could see, yet he had felt a sharp pain in his rear twice. He looked down and saw the two pebbles. He just couldn't understand it! He knew that pebbles don't fly about by themselves. He decided to keep an eye open for the culprit.

Just then Brer Bear came up. He had an armful of wood which he deposited on the ground. Turning to Brer Rabbit, he said, 'You haven't gathered any wood as yet, Brer Rabbit. You had better hurry. We will need lots of firewood to boil the tar.'

Brer Rabbit scratched his head. 'Yes, I know, but every time I bend down, pebbles keep hitting my rear. I can't understand it!'

'Let's see if it happens again,' said Brer Bear. 'In the meantime, I'll help you gather your share of the wood.'

Brer Anansi remained quite still up in the tree. He had to prevent himself from laughing by covering his mouth with his hand. 'Now,' he said quietly, 'I will wait a little and then shoot at Brer Rabbit again.'

Smack! Two minutes later Brer Rabbit felt another sting on his rear. He turned around quickly but saw no one. But he didn't look up in the tree.

'Well, that's that!' he said, and sat down on the ground. 'I refuse to get up or even move. Every time I bend down—Smack! I get it in the rear!'

Brer Bear did not believe him, though. 'I think that you are lying, Brer Rabbit. I think that you are playing tricks just to sit down to make me gather all the wood!'

'Of course not!' answered Brer Rabbit. 'Just you wait and see for yourself!'

Brer Bear continued gathering the fallen branches. He was nearly finished when something struck him from behind. He turned and glared at Brer Rabbit.

'Now you are pelting me to make it seem as if someone is really shooting at us!'

'Look, Brer Bear,' said Brer Rabbit, getting up and grabbing a big stick. 'I will teach you to believe what I say—'

'Eh? Is that so—' and Brer Bear too grabbed a big stick and advanced upon Brer Rabbit.

Up in the tree, Brer Anansi smiled. Good, he thought, his enemies were going to beat each other black-and-blue and all because of him.

But Brer Rabbit was not as stupid as Brer Anansi thought. No, he was much smarter!

'Brer Bear,' he said, 'I am not going to attack *you* with this stick. I mean to go and look for the culprit. He must be around somewhere.'

Brer Bear shrugged his shoulders. Anyway, he didn't feel like beating his friend. 'O.K., let's go and look for him. If we don't find him, you'll just have to gather all the wood!'

So the two friends separated and went into the surrounding bushes. Brer Anansi just smiled and waited.

Ten minutes later the two friends returned. They were both angry that they had wasted ten minutes.

'Come on, Brer Rabbit,' said Brer Bear, 'let's go and boil

the tar. If there was really someone shooting at—Ow!'

Brer Bear felt the sting in his rear, and said, 'If there's someone here, he's well hidden, but I'll find him!'

Up in the tree, Brer Anansi was so curious to see what was going on that he leant out too far and had to grab a branch or fall to his death. He managed to save himself but the catapult fell between Brer Rabbit's and Brer Bear's feet. The two friends looked up slowly and glared at Brer Anansi.

'So, it's you. I thought so,' said Brer Rabbit.

'Let's teach him a lesson,' said Brer Bear. 'Go bring the tar and pot here and we will do the boiling right here. We will set fire to the tree with all the extra wood!'

'Of course, we'll boil him in the tar when he falls down!' added Brer Rabbit gleefully as he ran off to fetch the tar and pot.

Brer Bear took two large stones from a nearby heap, placed them some six inches apart, and then heaped some dry branches underneath. He spread plenty of dry branches around the trunk of the tree and waited. Brer Rabbit came back with the pot full of tar and placed it on the stones. He then struck a match. Soon the tar was smoking away. With a lighted branch, he set fire to the other dry branches surrounding the tree.

Brer Anansi was now becoming afraid. He could not believe that his enemies would dare to burn him down. Now he was sure that they were even going to boil him in tar!

As the tar bubbled away, the bark of the tree became steadily blacker. Brer Bear sat on a heap of stones and stared at Brer Anansi. Brer Rabbit sat on a heap of dried branches repeating some calculations aloud.

'The tree is forty feet high and Brer Anansi is almost at

the top. The pot of tar is nearly forty feet from the foot of the tree. Therefore, when the tree falls, Brer Anansi will land straight into the pot of tar!'

Brer Anansi heard the calculations and knew that Brer Rabbit was correct. Brer Anansi would fall into the pot of boiling tar. But there was one factor that Brer Rabbit had not taken into account: the tree would hit the pot first if Brer Anansi leapt just as it started falling. He said to himself, 'I will wait until the tree is about to fall, and then I will jump and if I am lucky I may land on some dry branches!'

Before long, the tree creaked and toppled slowly to the ground. Brer Anansi leapt into the air and managed to avoid the pot of bubbling tar. He landed right on top of Brer Rabbit!

Meanwhile, as the tree crashed down to the ground, one of the thick branches landed on the edge of the pot and splashed the tar. Most of it landed on Brer Bear. He was black from head to toe, but luckily, he was only singed because of his thick fur. Howling and dancing about, Brer Bear managed to get one of his big feet stuck in the tar pot. He hopped about, making even more noise with the pot banging on the stones.

Brer Rabbit had recovered himself in the meantime and grabbed Brer Anansi who promptly let loose with all four pairs of his limbs. What a fight!

Slap! Slam! Pow! Oof! went Brer Anansi and Brer Rabbit. On top of that, the pot stuck on Brer Bear's foot clanged Boing! Boing! What a racket they all made!

Before long every animal in the forest for miles around had gathered around the three 'musicians'. They looked on in awed silence.

'What's going on here?' demanded a big bass voice.

Brer Anansi and Brer Rabbit stopped fighting at once. Brer Bear too stopped knocking the pot about and they all looked guiltily at the King of the Animals.

'Well?' demanded King Leo. 'I asked a question, didn't I?'

'Yes, sire,' said Brer Bear. 'I was just boiling tar when Brer Anansi came along—'

'—No, he's lying,' interrupted Brer Anansi. 'I was here first when Brer Rabbit came along and wanted to boil—'

'—No, no! You're the liar, Brer Anansi!' shouted Brer Rabbit.

And all three of them shouted at the same time!

'Silence!' demanded King Leo. 'Let's hear all this from the beginning.'

The King turned to Brer Bear. 'Just who are you, by the way?'

Brer Bear was black all over. Only his eyes were showing. Yes, just who is he? thought the rest of the animals. They had never seen anyone so black before except, of course, Brer Anansi.

'I am Brer Bear, sire,' said Brer Bear. 'I'm like this because this no-good Brer Anansi—'

'O.K., Brer Bear,' said King Leo, 'let's hear the story right from the beginning.'

Brer Bear sat down on the tar stained rocks and told his story. After he had finished, King Leo took up the catapult from the ground and turned his fierce gaze on Brer Anansi.

Brer Anansi trembled. He knew that he was in for it. He was going to be punished. Then King Leo turned abruptly to Brer Bear and Brer Rabbit.

'You three are always larking about. I'll have to stop this once and for all. I banish all three of you from this forest for three years!'

A murmur went up amongst the animals. Brer Anansi, Brer Bear and Brer Rabbit stared at each other in astonishment. They never thought that it would end like this. Banished from the forest by the King?

Brer Bear was very angry. He stamped his foot hard down on the ground. The pot flew off and landed with a sharp klunk on Brer Rabbit's head. A bump grew that was even bigger than his own ears put together!

How everyone laughed and laughed. They all had tears in their eyes. Everyone, that is, except Brer Rabbit who looked miserable. Even his friend, Brer Bear, was laughing at him. Eventually, the laughter died down and King Leo spoke.

'I have never laughed so much in my life before, and to show you three how pleased I am, I will reverse the punishment I passed a few minutes ago.'

The three animals smiled. Even Brer Rabbit was no longer angry.

'Instead,' continued King Leo, 'I will give each of you a spade and some work to do!'

The two friends and Brer Anansi could not protest. They were led off and each given a spade to dig a twenty-square-yard hole of about twenty feet deep. The King wanted to build a swimming pool!

So the three animals got down to the digging. The earth was hard, very hard, and the three of them sweated. How angry they were! Brer Bear and Brer Rabbit were the angriest of the three. They stamped their feet and ground their teeth at Brer Anansi.

'You just wait until we get out of here, friend, and we'll show you where barley grows!'

'Yes,' added Brer Rabbit, 'we will even show you where pickled onions grow too!'

Brer Anansi did not bother with them. He was saving all his strength to make a dash for it when the digging was over.

They finished the ditch late that night and handed back the spades. The chase was on! Brer Anansi ran for home with Brer Bear and Brer Rabbit coming after for all they were worth. It was dark so they could hardly see where they were going. It was even more difficult for Brer Anansi to see Brer Bear who was as black as the night with all the tar on his fur.

Then the rain came down. It rained and rained and rained. Brer Anansi was wet and miserable as he ran home. He climbed up his silk rope and was safe. All night long the rain continued.

The next morning King Leo was surprised to see his swimming pool half-filled with water. He was even more surprised to see Brer Bear and Brer Rabbit swimming about in it. They had fallen in during the night on their way home and could not get out!

The Rainbow War

'Citizens of Animal Land!' shouted Brer Monkey at the market place one Saturday. 'Hear Ye! Hear Ye! An announcement from the King! An announcement!'

No one bothered with him. They were all too busy among themselves, buying and selling, to listen to Brer Monkey. Even Brer Rabbit and Brer Bear were buying, which they rarely did. The two friends were begging the squirrel to lower the price of nuts from a silver coin for seven to half a silver coin for four. After ten minutes of explaining the rules of salesmanship, they managed to fool the squirrel into agreeing to their price; upon which Brer Bear took out ten silver coins and proceeded to buy nuts at four for half a silver coin.

Brer Monkey, meanwhile, realized that no one would listen to him. They were only interested in buying and selling. In making a profit!

'Talk about something free,' suggested Brer Anansi, who was standing next to Brer Monkey who was standing on a barrel. 'They are sure to crowd around all right.'

Brer Anansi waited patiently to hear the announcement. He knew that the King had a knack for giving away prizes at various contests and he, Brer Anansi, had a knack for winning these prizes. He was sure that Brer Monkey had some kind of contest to talk about.

'Listen! Listen! Listen!' shouted Brer Monkey. 'Prizes! Prizes! Prizes!'

That did it! In two seconds Brer Monkey was surrounded by all the animals in the market place.

'Go on,' said Brer Bear. 'Let's hear about the prizes.'

'Yes, tell us, and let me go and win it all. Come on, let's hear of it!' joined in Brer Rabbit. 'We're waiting.'

'Hear ye! Hear ye! Hear ye!' began Brer Monkey. 'The King, His Gracious Majesty, King Leo the First, most noble, proud, generous, forgiving, gracious etc. etc. is organizing a New Contest! It is to be a yearly feature! It is to be called "The Best-Decorated House of the Year".'

'Bah,' grumbled Brer Bear. 'Nothing but work in that! Not for me! Bah!'

'And the prizes?' asked Brer Rabbit.

'There are three,' shouted Brer Monkey, who was the King's chief messenger. 'First Prize, two barrels of imported syrup brought specially from Shanghai by Special Order of the King!'

There was a loud gasp of wonder from the animals when they heard this. What a prize! Shanghai syrup was the finest in the world!

'Second Prize,' continued Brer Monkey, 'is a barrow of Indian cloves from the Eastern State of India!'

There was another gasp! That too was a priceless gift! Cloves! One could put cloves into almost anything! It was a great flavouring!

'Third Prize!' concluded Brer Monkey. 'This is a flask of perfume from Florence!'

There was another gasp. Everyone nodded. What prizes! Oh, if they could each have a whiff of perfume they would all be satisfied!

While they were talking, Brer Anansi was making off with Brer Bear and Brer Rabbit's barrow of already-purchased nuts. He had heard the first prize alone and was satisfied. He wanted the first prize!

Brer Anansi sold the nuts very cheaply to Brer Weasel and bought a tin of every paint that was in stock. Paints were sold cheaply because no one had bought any in a long time, and buying all the available paint from the shop he was sure that he alone would have the Best Decorated House!

Half an hour later Brer Anansi stood in his house surveying his tins of paint. He had about eight pots of paint to decorate his house with. They were of every colour: red, blue, green, black, brown, purple, pink and even silver. They were the only paints that the shop had. The rest of the animals would have to go to the next territory to buy paint. Even Brer Bear and Brer Rabbit would be finding it difficult.

But there was one problem. Brer Anansi had to decide which paint to start his decoration with. Should he use red or blue? Then again, how about pink, black or silver?

While he was deciding, who happened along but his two

enemies! Brer Rabbit and Brer Bear guessed that Brer Anansi must have stolen their barrow of nuts, so they came quietly up to his tree-house on a ladder to punish him.

Brer Anansi did not notice them. He was busy muttering to himself about which paint he should use first.

Brer Bear crept up first and behind him came Brer Rabbit. Brer Bear picked up a pot of black paint and took off the lid. He was going to throw the paint on Brer Anansi! He lifted the pot up and prepared to throw, but he lifted it too high and the paint fell over behind his back. Brer Rabbit, who was just behind, was soaked in black paint! How black and angry he looked!

Brer Anansi turned around when he heard the splash. He was most surprised to see his two enemies inside his house. They had found a way of coming up! He was even more surprised to see Brer Rabbit black all over, and Brer Bear looking so helplessly at his friend.

'Oho!' exclaimed Brer Rabbit. 'So you are at it again, you clumsy oaf! I will teach you!' And before anyone knew what was what, Brer Rabbit had seized a pot of green paint and splashed it over Brer Bear.

Brer Anansi was fearful that his paints would be finished and his house would be in a great mess, so he dashed forward to get rid of his two enemies. Of course Brer Bear and Brer Rabbit refused to go—and as usual a fight started. A full-scale battle and the ammunition was paint!

Splash! Splash! A dash of red here, some green there, a dab of pink, a little black and some of the other colours. Paint was sprayed almost everywhere. The walls had the most!

'Paint Brer Anansi!' shouted Brer Bear. 'Throw some green down his throat! Red his great black hide!'

'And some yellow across his back for the coward he is!'

added Brer Rabbit. 'A long broad stripe of yellow!'

Brer Anansi was most angry. 'A coward?' he shouted back. 'I will teach you two a lesson, you oafs!'

Without even thinking that he was in his own house. Brer Anansi scooped up the paint that had fallen in pools on the floor and splashed it at his two enemies. The battle was resumed! In two minutes the walls looked as if a hundred rainbows had gone mad across the skies!

Soon there was no more paint left to splash about with. Brer Anansi was as eager as ever to fight. He seized four empty pots in four of his limbs and let fly as if he was fighting Mr Thunder for his very life! His two enemies could stand it no longer. They were seeing colours all around! Brer Bear ran out, with Brer Rabbit close behind.

'Remember the ladder!' shouted Brer Rabbit.

But it was too late. Brer Bear forgot he came up on a ladder, and stepped hurriedly forward. He fell right to the bottom of the tree and landed with a sharp thump on his rear!

'Yeow!' he yelled.

Brer Rabbit remembered the ladder all right, but he didn't remember that the middle rung was missing. He climbed half-way down, and was sent tumbling down the other half!

The ladder slid down next. One end landed straight on Brer Bear, which fastened his head neatly between two rungs at the other end of the ladder!

Down the tree came the four pots. They landed hard on the two friends. They both climbed to their feet and howled away into the day with the ladder fastened between them.

Brer Anansi couldn't help laughing! There were his two enemies howling away like mad, as if they were clowns going to put out a fire in a great circus show! How he laughed and laughed! It certainly was good fun!

'May we come up?'

Brer Anansi stopped laughing. He looked down. Below, there were three animals dressed in their tweed suits: the Owl, the Racoon and the Beaver.

'We are the judges of the "Best Decorated House of the Year",' explained the Owl. 'May we come up and inspect your house?'

'Is the contest time up already?'

'Of course!' said the Racoon. 'It is now five o'clock. Didn't Brer Monkey tell you that the closing time was four?'

Brer Anansi had not heard the rules. He had left while Brer Monkey was telling the animals the second and third prizes.

'Enough of this chattering,' said the Beaver. 'Throw down your rope ladder. We're coming up!'

There was nothing for it but to throw the rope ladder down. He couldn't refuse the King's Judges. The three animals soon climbed up. They set about examining the walls immediately.

'Oh my!' exclaimed the Owl. 'What is this? Oh, what colours! What design! What arrangement!'

'A certainly agreeable composition,' agreed the Racoon. 'It shows the hand of a Great Artist!'

The three judges were *admiring* the paint splashes on the wall! They thought that it was Brer Anansi's decorating skill!

'There can be no doubt,' concluded the Owl, 'that Brer Anansi has won the First Prize!'

Brer Anansi was most surprised. What a stroke of luck! His two enemies had done him a great turn after all.

Hooray for them!

He could imagine Brer Rabbit and Brer Bear still running with the ladder between them!

Brer Anansi took up his towel to clean himself for the presentation. He stopped a second later and threw the towel in a corner. He would go just as he was—coated in many colours—to collect the First Prize for the 'Best Decorated House of the Year'!

Disappearing Act

Brer Anansi stopped abruptly. A big notice caught his eye. It was on a large sheet of cardboard nailed to a tree. He inspected the notice carefully. It read

ATTENTION! ATTENTION! ATTENTION! THE GREAT MAGICIAN PRESTO WILL VISIT ANIMAL LAND FOR A ONE-EVENING ENGAGEMENT. HIS ASSISTANT VANISHO WILL BE ALSO PRESENT! COME AND SEE THE GREAT DISAPPEARING ACT!

JUGGLING! THE ROPE TO HEAVEN! THE FIERY DRAGON FROM HELL! ENTRANCE FEE: ONE SILVER COIN! COMING WEDNESDAY IN FARMER BROWN'S BURNT-OUT CORNFIELD.
P.S. IF YOU ARE PRESENT AND ARE NOT SATISFIED AFTER THE SHOW IS OVER, YOUR MONEY WILL BE GLADLY REFUNDED!

Brer Anansi smiled. He liked magic! He would gladly pay a silver coin to see the show!

He met Brer Weasel just outside his shop.

'Good morning to you,' said Brer Weasel. 'My, you do look happy!'

'Of course! Of course!' exclaimed Brer Anansi. 'I am happy! I am going to enjoy this coming Wednesday evening's entertainment!'

'Indeed!' said Brer Weasel. 'I will be there too. I hear it will be a great show!'

'I hope so,' said Brer Anansi. 'But who are Presto and Vanisho?'

'I don't know myself,' explained Brer Weasel. 'But I think Brer Rabbit knows. He bought a keg of nails from me and said that Presto had commissioned him to make a stage.'

'Ah, a stage!' exclaimed Brer Anansi, joyfully. 'Then everyone will be able to see easily. I must go and watch the building of the stage. Have to get a good seat, you know.'

'So long, Brer Anansi,' said Brer Weasel. 'Select a good seat for me too!'

'Of course! Of course!'

Brer Anansi left quickly. He was going to inspect the burnt-out cornfield. He realized that something was odd. His two enemies never worked for anything, not even money. They were too lazy for that.

They must be getting free tickets, thought Brer Anansi. I had better go and see how the work is progressing. My, what a show this is going to be! A proper stage! Indeed!

He stopped just near to the blackened cornfield and hid behind a tree. He did not want his two enemies to see him. He quietly watched what was going on. Brer Bear and Brer Rabbit were building a stage. It was going to be big. It was five feet high and about twenty feet square.

Brer Anansi listened hard to what was happening. Brer Rabbit was speaking.

'By six o'clock we will have the stage ready.'

'If we had made it smaller,' complained Brer Bear, digging a post hole, 'there would have been less work.'

'But you don't understand,' explained Brer Rabbit. 'A bigger stage would reflect a great performance! The animals will see a big stage and they will be impressed! They will all think that it is going to be a truly great show! Keep digging!'

Brer Bear stopped a minute to wipe the sweat off his face. 'It sure is hard work.'

Brer Anansi was not interested. He turned to go, but what Brer Rabbit said next made him stop.

'We will make about a hundred silver coins from the show!'

A hundred? Brer Anansi was puzzled. Who would give away a hundred coins just to make a stage? Fifteen silver coins were enough to get a stage built, including the cost of boards and the keg of nails.

It would have been better, thought Brer Anansi, if I had offered to make the stage for Presto; I would have asked for, say, about eighty silver coins. But the spider did not know who Presto was.

'It is a good idea,' said Brer Bear, 'to fool the animals. We will get the tunnel dug like you said, under the stage and out of the field. When the performance starts, we will take the money, open the trapdoor on the stage and crawl away through the tunnel!'

'Ho-ho!' laughed Brer Rabbit. 'They will think that Presto and Vanisho have disappeared for good!'

Brer Anansi was taken aback at this. What a mean trick!

'We will never return to Animal Land,' said Brer Bear. 'With the money we will go away for good. Good riddance to everybody! Good riddance to King Leo and his laws! Good riddance to Brer Anansi!'

'Shee!' whispered Brer Rabbit, looking around. He did not see Brer Anansi. 'Not so loud. We musn't let anyone hear. This is a great risk. If they catch us, we will be tarred alive. Do be careful what you say, Brer Bear.'

Brer Bear looked around too. 'I'm sorry. It won't happen again.'

'Good!' said Brer Rabbit. 'Keep working! I have never been so happy in my life before—working that is!'

Brer Anansi went home immediately. He was most humiliated! His two enemies were going to perform a very nasty trick, and everyone will each pay a silver coin for something they won't get! He sat on his bed with his chin in his hands. His enemies were going away! They would be going away with about a hundred silver coins. It would be good if his enemies left, but not with his money! Brer Anansi leaped to his feet and clenched his fists in the air!

'They won't get away with it!' exclaimed the enraged Brer Anansi. 'It is going to be their last trick! They will be sorry for it! Every animal who attends the performance will make them pay for it!'

He sat down again to think of a plan to surprise his two

87

enemies at their own game. He thought carefully, considering every aspect of his plot, and in about ten minutes, sure enough, he had a fool-proof plan. It was a great plan! His best plan! A plan that would cause lots of laughter for the audience who would attend the Magic Show!

On Wednesday afternoon, all the animals were assembled around the stage. The show was about to start. The money that Brer Rabbit had collected was in a small bag tied to his waist. They were about to perform their tricks.

But Brer Anansi and Brer Weasel were not present. Instead, who turned up but King Leo. He even paid five silver coins and came on one of his golden thrones, surrounded by his four massive Court Gorillas. He too had turned up to see some magic!

The show started. First Brer Rabbit, who had his head covered in a white turban and wore a long silver cloak with black stars on it, made a low bow. His friend, Brer Bear, had had his fur dyed a pale yellow and he had on a black mask. None of the animals knew or suspected that Brer Rabbit and Brer Bear were the two magicians. Well, except Brer Anansi, but he was not in sight.

'I, Presto,' said Brer Rabbit, 'am a great magician! Myself and my assistant, Vanisho,' Brer Bear made a low bow, 'will now deliver some fine magnificent stunts!'

Everyone clapped.

Brer Rabbit pointed to a box on the stage. 'I will now put Vanisho under the box and say the magic words. He will disappear!'

Brer Bear went under the box. The stage was a few inches above the heads of the animals so they could not see the trapdoor. Besides, it was covered by a five-cornered box.

'And now,' said Brer Rabbit, 'the magic words!' He waved his stick three times over the box and muttered

'*Xlyczayb! Oyahostoka! Galla-go-gella! Prattakashka-Alabush!*'

Then he lifted the box up.

All the animals gasped! Vanisho had really vanished!

In fact, Vanisho had opened the trapdoor and was covered by the stage. Everyone present thought that he had really disappeared.

'Now!' exclaimed Brer Rabbit. 'I will bring Vanisho back! Just look as I utter the magic words again! *Ah-la-la-hushkay! La, le-le!*'

Then he raised the box up. What a shock he got! No Vanisho was to be seen! Brer Rabbit realized that Brer Bear had forgotten the plan the two of them had made earlier. Brer Bear was supposed to have crawled out through the tunnel on the second act and not the first.

'Ahem!' Brer Rabbit stamped his foot hard on the stage. He really did it to call back Brer Bear, whom he imagined to be half-way through the tunnel by then. He turned the box down again over the trapdoor.

'Now I will bring him back finally!'

He muttered the magic words again and raised the box. Still there was no Vanisho to be seen. All the animals were now giggling. Brer Rabbit did not like it.

'All right! All right!' He stamped his foot again. A thud sounded from under the stage. Only Brer Rabbit heard it. He smiled.

'Okay, I will finally bring him back this time!'

He muttered a whole paragraph of magic words. Then he waved his wand about twenty times. All the animals held their breath. Brer Rabbit lifted the box up.

Under it he saw Brer Weasel!

All the animals giggled. Good King Leo roared with laughter. The other animals could not help but join in!

Everyone laughed except Brer Rabbit, who appeared shocked, and Brer Weasel, who looked most astonished.

But Brer Rabbit was most annoyed. He could not understand what had happened. He knew that his magic certainly was not magic. He had really muttered a string of nonsense but it had worked. Now he was in real trouble!

The animals were really enjoying the show, much to Presto's annoyance. He wanted to be off quickly with the silver coins!

'A mistake! A rather humorous mistake!' he exclaimed. 'A really serious complication, but watch me bring Vanisho back!'

He did not know what was going on, but he wanted to make an attempt to produce Brer Bear before the animals demanded their coins back and laughed him off the stage. This time he roared out a whole page of magic words. Then he lifted the box. There was no one underneath! All the animals now gasped. What magic!

Even the magician himself was most surprised. Now he was getting excited. He thought that he was really a magician after all. He smiled.

'Now watch! Here comes Vanisho!'

He muttered a little more than a page of strange words and waved his wand until his arm ached. He smiled to the audience, and made a bow. Then he lifted the box up.

What a shock he got! Seated cross-legged where the box had been was Brer Anansi. How the animals laughed. What fun! Here certainly was a mixed-up magician. Brer Rabbit fumed and stamped his feet. How angry he was! He hurriedly covered Brer Anansi with the box and started waving his wand about. The animals were still laughing. Brer Rabbit opened the box a little and took a peep at Brer Anansi.

'Look,' he said. 'Get Brer Bear back and I will give you twenty silver coins!'

But Brer Anansi only stuck out his tongue at his enemy. Brer Rabbit hastily increased his offer to fifty silver coins. But Brer Anansi only pulled the box down. Brer Rabbit stood up and took out his spotted handkerchief. He wiped the sweat off his face. All the animals were laughing; even King Leo had stopped sipping his lemonade and was enjoying himself. How he roared and shook himself about in his chair! What fun!

Brer Rabbit realized that Brer Anansi was somehow responsible for his plight. He inwardly hoped that Brer Anansi would bring Brer Bear back. He probably had him tied and gagged under the stage.

He muttered some more magic words, and added, softly, 'Please, Brer Anansi, bring Brer Bear back or I will be ruined.'

He waved his wand three times and lifted the box up. He was most surprised to see Brer Anansi and Brer Weasel seated on the closed trapdoor! There was a fresh outburst of laughter! Presto was certainly a queer magician.

How frustrated and angry Brer Rabbit was! How he stamped his feet and ground his many teeth together and went around in numerous circles! He really was an angry rabbit!

'Now!' he shouted, at the top of his voice. 'This has gone too far!' All the animals became serious and looked on with rapt attention almost immediately. 'I will bring Brer Bear back!'

Everyone gasped! Brer Bear? What was Presto saying? His assistant was certainly Vanisho. Was he going mad over his own magic?

The box was turned over the trapdoor, and this time

Presto sat on it! He sat on it for full ten minutes and shouted all sorts of words! Then he stood up and raised the box. There was no one underneath! Brer Bear had disappeared first! Then went Brer Weasel! Now Brer Anansi was gone! Brer Rabbit was so fatigued, frustrated and overworked, that he sat down on the box, threw his wand aside and started to cry!

Five minutes later he was still crying. Brer Anansi opened the trapdoor and came out. Brer Weasel too came out. Last of all came Brer Bear, who was certainly looking afraid!

Then Brer Anansi explained what had happened. He told the animals how he had overheard what his two enemies had said, and how he went and told Brer Weasel all about it. Then he and Brer Weasel had hid under the stage and made a wreck of Brer Rabbit's plan.

Everyone laughed! It certainly had been good fun! What a lovely time they had had; well, all except Brer Rabbit and Brer Bear. The King spoke.

'All right. We all had our fun but someone must pay. Let us give Brer Anansi and Brer Weasel the silver coins. They must divide them equally, fifty each. We are thanking them for having captured two rogues and making us all laugh at the same time!'

Everyone clapped. Then King Leo turned to the two friends. 'Brer Bear and Brer Rabbit, you two ought to be ashamed of yourselves! Two swindlers, that's what you are. Two swindlers. But I'll be lenient this time. We will all go home and leave Presto and Vanisho to break down the stage they built and take the boards back to their homes. That is punishment enough. I hope they learn from their lesson!'

Everyone left. Brer Anansi and Brer Weasel left too. Only Presto and Vanisho remained to dismantle the stage they had worked so hard to build. How sad they were. But it served them right, and it was thanks to the smart Brer Anansi that they were rightly punished, announced the Owl.

Brer Anansi, meanwhile, went home and started counting his fifty silver coins for the eleventh time!

The Missing Voice

One Thursday morning, Brer Anansi woke up half an hour earlier than usual. He opened his door at about nine o'clock, and poked his head out.

What a shock he got! It was the greatest shock he had ever received before in his entire life. It was a downright unexpected shock! It completely unnerved him! How he trembled in fright!

Right at the bottom of his tree-house, who could be seen sitting there but Mr Thunder!

How Brer Anansi wished he were somewhere else! He remembered how he had tricked Mr Thunder some time ago into taking a slap from him. Now Mr Thunder was going to return the slap! Brer Anansi's many knees started knocking together. His teeth also started chattering. What a noise! Poor Brer Anansi nearly died with fright. Now Mr Thunder was calling him down! He was so confused that he could not think of going down! He never even thought of running.

Besides, Mr Thunder was down below and there was simply no place he could run to in safety. Mr Thunder beckoned again! Brer Anansi found sufficient courage to step forward. He held on to his tree rope and prepared to swing down. Then came a crash!

Brer Anansi nearly jumped out of his skin! What was that? But it was only the wind blowing the door shut. The spider reluctantly slid down inch by inch to Mr Thunder waiting below for him. This looked like the end of Brer Anansi! He had met his match at last!

He stood shivering at the feet of Mr Thunder! What big feet! What a big body! What a big mouth! And what big hands! Brer Anansi's heart felt like a lump of rotten potato. What was going to happen to him?

Much to his surprise, Mr Thunder took out a notebook and started writing something. Brer Anansi looked on quietly, half afraid, half puzzled. What was going on? Mr Thunder stopped writing and handed the book to Brer Anansi. The spider stretched out a shaking hand and took the notebook. Mr Thunder nodded.

Brer Anansi read what had been written down. He just could not believe it! He rubbed his eyes and read again. Then he looked up at Mr Thunder. So that was it!

The note read, '*I have lost my voice, Brer Anansi. You have got to help me find it!*'

That accounted for Mr Thunder's silence! It was almost unbelievable! The great Mr Thunder without a voice?

A doubt crossed Brer Anansi's mind...was it a trick?

As if reading the spider's mind, Mr Thunder took back his notebook and turned a page. He wrote steadily for about two minutes. Brer Anansi took the book when Mr Thunder had finished.

He read, '*This is no trick. I lost my voice last night at Echo Valley in the next country and I can't find it. If you help me get it back before anyone finds out, I will give you anything you want.*'

Brer Anansi was suddenly no longer afraid. Mr Thunder would give him anything he wanted! He would at that, too!

'Mr Thunder!' said Brer Anansi. 'Will you give me anything I want if I help you find your voice?'

Mr Thunder nodded.

'Anything?' repeated Brer Anansi.

Again Mr Thunder nodded.

Brer Anansi smiled. 'Okay, I'll help you. Now suppose you tell me all that happened last night. Go on, write it down, and I will tell you where you can find your voice.'

Mr Thunder started writing quickly. He filled pages and pages. In the meantime, Brer Anansi wondered about what he should ask for. A house on the highest cloud would do him a heap of good. Brer Bear and Brer Rabbit would not catch him there. But he himself would not be able to reach anybody. He had to think again. He had to think of a strange, novel, priceless and only-one-of-its-kind gift! Here was his chance to become rich! His only chance in a lifetime! He won't be caught lying down. Oh, no! The great Brer Anansi was going to grasp opportunity with all his eight limbs!

Mr Thunder finished writing and handed Brer Anansi the notebook. Brer Anansi read through the eleven pages very slowly. It took him thirty minutes. He could not find the cure! He read through the pages once more.

Every time he looked up to turn a page he found Mr Thunder's eyes on him. How fierce Mr Thunder looked. His eyes seemed to say: 'You trick me this time, Brer Anansi and I will swallow you, your home and all, in one gulp!'

Then Brer Anansi suddenly realized why and where Mr Thunder had lost his voice! He also realized that it would only take Mr Thunder a few days to recover his voice. It was a simple matter: five or six days at least. Even seven days!

But Brer Anansi did not tell Mr Thunder this! He realized that if the animals knew that Mr Thunder had lost his voice, Mr Thunder's reputation would be ruined. No one would respect him after that, whether he recovered his voice or not, and he would soon be out of business. Mr Thunder had come to the spider for help because Brer Anansi was afraid of him. He would not dare tell a soul what had happened.

'Ah!' exclaimed Brer Anansi. 'This is a very tricky mystery. I dare say even the greatest doctor in Animal Land would find it hard to assist!'

Mr Thunder looked most annoyed at this.

'However!' Brer Anansi held a hand up. 'You must have no fear! I, Brer Anansi, shall help!'

Mr Thunder smiled.

Brer Anansi continued. 'I shall ask a personal favour in lieu of my fee. I shall ask for a dozen thunderbolts when I cure your illness!'

What a strange request! But Brer Anansi was using his head. A dozen thunderbolts would make him a king. All he had to do was drop a thunderbolt between Brer Bear and Brer Rabbit and that did take care of them for good. He could use the other eleven on the animals who opposed him when he appointed himself Emperor!

Mr Thunder agreed to the twelve thunderbolts. Brer Anansi told him to return on Monday and he would have his voice all nice and ready for him. Mr Thunder left with a smile on his broad, rough face. He would be well in a few days, he thought, and no one would be the wiser!

But he did not know that Brer Anansi had had one of his big ideas as usual. He was up to one of his big schemes!

Monday Morning saw Mr Thunder back at Brer Anansi's house. Brer Anansi came down to him and smiled. Mr Thunder did not smile back!

Brer Anansi realized that something had gone wrong. He had thought that Mr Thunder had shouted all Wednesday night at Echo Valley to amuse himself and he had ended up hoarse. Brer Anansi had reasoned that in a few days Mr Thunder's voice would come back by itself. Now Mr Thunder was angry. He wanted his voice back immediately! It was a lucky thing that he had not given Brer Anansi his dozen thunderbolts.

'I know,' protested Brer Anansi hastily. 'Your tongue! Stick it out!'

Mr Thunder opened his mouth and Brer Anansi examined it, muttering, 'Ah, ah! Still too light! Yes, a day...a day, yes. One more day will do it!'

So Mr Thunder promised in writing to come back the next day to have his voice back. It was agreed upon between doctor and patient that the patient should bring the thunderbolts with him...

Tuesday morning saw an enraged Mr Thunder outside Brer Anansi's house. He had not recovered his voice and he had come to deal with Brer Anansi. As soon as the crafty spider saw Mr Thunder coming down the road without his thunderbolts, he realized what had happened, so he ran away to hide for a few weeks until Mr Thunder forgot all about him.

And did Mr Thunder recover his voice? You can be sure he did! Listen when the sky is cloudy and it rains a lot, and you will be sure to hear him. You may even see the thunderbolts that Brer Anansi had tried to obtain for himself!

Anansi's Picnic

Early one morning, just as the sun had started its long climb across the skies, Brer Anansi took his lunch basket and oars. He was going on a picnic on the island in the middle of the river.

It was a bright morning. The sky was full of little white feathery clouds, the air was fresh, and the wind was blowing softly through the trees. Brer Anansi felt happy. It was a good morning. It was a most agreeable morning. He stopped to listen for a moment to the cheerful sounds the birds were making. Here and there fluttered a white butterfly. Brer Anansi smiled. A big, wide smile. It was a smile of great happiness. He was not going to let anything spoil his morning!

In ten minutes he came to the jetty, where he set about launching his row-boat which was almost out of the water. Then he set about bailing the little pool of water that had collected at the bottom from the rain and waves.

Suddenly he heard a noise: the great tramping of many big feet. He looked up. Coming down the jetty were his two enemies with a great big lunch basket between them. Brer Rabbit and Brer Bear were also going on a picnic!

Both his enemies stopped when they saw him. 'Well, well!' exclaimed Brer Bear. 'Look what we have here! If it isn't Brer Anansi!'

'Ah, it is Brer Anansi,' joined in Brer Rabbit. 'Didn't I tell you that he did be here! I thought I smelled him in the air! The musty smell of corruption! The cold smell of devilry! The itching smell of one so long accustomed to dwell in the slime and muck of stupidity!'

Brer Anansi stopped bailing his boat, for a second or two. They were insulting him. He looked at them some seconds more. They were standing at the edge of the jetty, heads twisted a little to one side and eyes full of mischief.

Brer Anansi smiled, and he turned back to bailing his boat. Today was his happy day, and he would not let anyone spoil it. Prevention is better than cure, he had been told many times by the Owl. No, he wouldn't let anyone spoil his happiness!

Brer Rabbit and Brer Bear did not know what to make of it all. They were most surprised. There they were, insulting their enemy and all he did was just smile back!

'He is so stupid,' added Brer Bear, 'that he does not know

an insult when he hears one!'

Brer Anansi did not bother with them. He finished bailing his boat and placed his lunch and oars inside.

'Do you know what we are taking with us, Brer Anansi?' asked Brer Bear. 'Would you like to know?'

There was no answer.

'Well,' continued Brer Bear. 'Since you are so shy at asking, I will tell you. We are taking chicken with potatoes and butter, tomato gravy, sliced fruit-cake, pudding, banana pies, meat pies, all-kinds-of-pies, lemonade, pepper sauce, pickled onions, stewed fish cutlets, and for dessert we will have...'

But he got no further. Brer Anansi was some yards away in his boat, heading for the island. He had ignored his two enemies completely! The two friends couldn't stand it. They felt humiliated! Insulted! Frustrated! And certainly annoyed! They dumped their lunch baskets into the boat, seized their oars and launched themselves speedily after Brer Anansi!

They soon caught up with him because Brer Anansi was cruising slowly along. Brer Rabbit steered the boat alongside Brer Anansi's. There was a gap, however, of some yards in between. The two friends were taking no chances.

'And for dessert we will have,' continued Brer Bear, 'tinned pear cooled at the bottom of a deep hole filled with water; next we will eat our cocoa-chocolate fudge and drink apple sauce!'

There was a great deal of silence after this: they were waiting for Brer Anansi to say something. They thought that Brer Anansi was going to boast about what he had brought along. Brer Anansi said nothing.

'What will you have, Brer Anansi?' asked Brer Bear, who could stand the silence no longer.

Still Brer Anansi said nothing. Both his enemies began to look closely at him. Was he sick? Was something wrong with him? Why was he so silent? Brer Anansi silent? They couldn't understand it. Even Brer Rabbit couldn't understand what was going on. Then all of a sudden Brer Anansi started humming. Brer Bear and Brer Rabbit looked at each other in amazement. Was he mad?

There was only one way of finding out. Brer Anansi had never in his life ignored a challenge. Brer Rabbit was going to try him out.

'Brer Anansi!' shouted Brer Rabbit. 'How about a contest? I, Brer Rabbit, hereby challenge you to a Boat-Race!'

'Hooray! A Boat-Race!' cried Brer Bear, who was feeling joyfully energetic. 'A Boat-Race for us! Let's go!'

'One, two three, go!' exclaimed Brer Rabbit. 'We're off!'

How fast the two friends went! In two paddle strokes each they were well in front of Brer Anansi! How they shot forward! How fast they went!

They had almost reached the island which was about three miles from their starting point when Brer Rabbit eventually realized that Brer Anansi was not in the race!

'Stop! Stop!' cried Brer Rabbit.

He and Brer Bear looked back. Brer Anansi's boat was a little dot behind. The two friends looked at each other stupidly: they were racing themselves after all! How annoyed they felt!

'Let's give up,' said Brer Bear. 'I *am* tired. How about some lemonade?'

'No!' cried Brer Rabbit. 'We are going to have the lemonade with the lunch!'

'Then let's have lunch now,' insisted Brer Bear.

'No!' shouted Brer Rabbit. 'We will eat later. It is only

about nine o'clock now. We have about four hours to go.'

'Four hours!' howled Brer Bear. 'Oh, me! I am starving! I sure will die of exhaustion long before then!'

'Oh, well, all right!' Brer Bear smiled when Brer Rabbit said this. 'Have some river water.' Brer Bear looked sour once more. 'Mind you, don't drink plenty or there will be no room in your stomach for the food.'

Of course, Brer Bear couldn't drink the muddy river water. He couldn't drink anything if Brer Rabbit would not give it to him. Although half the food was his, he was afraid to take anything. He realized that it was Brer Rabbit's boat, and if he argued too much Brer Rabbit might throw him overboard. He waited in silence.

'Seeing you are so tired,' offered Brer Rabbit, 'we will wait here for Brer Anansi. No sense in going back all the way to tease him. But I tell you, I am not yet finished with him! In fact, we have hardly begun!'

So the two friends waited silently in their boat. Fifteen minutes they waited. Brer Anansi's boat soon came up to theirs and it went past without Brer Anansi saying anything.

Brer Anansi wanted to say, 'Having engine trouble, I see,' but on second thoughts he decided to keep his mouth shut. But not Brer Rabbit. Their boat followed alongside Brer Anansi's.

'Ah, you finally got here,' began Brer Rabbit. 'What a slow-coach! I have to tell Brer Tortoise that he has a rival! A rival for travelling slowly. Keep it up, Brer Anansi, and you did be the slowest Brer Animal in the world!'

Brer Anansi said nothing.

'Let's ram him,' proposed Brer Bear. 'We will paddle a long way off and then head straight for him. If he does not steer out of the way, he will end up at the bottom of the river, food hamper and all!'

'Ah capital! Capital!' Brer Rabbit smiled. He realized that the food basket would float and they could grab it up. Brer Anansi was a good cook—well, sort of—and he was sure to have lots to eat.

'Okay, Brer Anansi!' exclaimed both friends together. 'Watch out! Ha-ha!'

Brer Rabbit and Brer Bear paddled a long way off and turned the canoe around. What a shock they got! Brer Anansi had disappeared. There was no boat, no Brer Anansi or food hamper to be seen. They could only see a large, close island and a creek. While they had been paddling back to take a good run at him, Brer Anansi had reached the creek, and when both friends stopped and turned back, Brer Anansi's boat was already tied up there.

Brer Rabbit was in a terrible rage. It certainly wasn't his morning! Things were, indeed, going badly for him. Brer Bear was now nearly exhausted. He had been exerting himself and all for nothing. Sure enough, he was in the middle of the boat and had two oars for paddling. Brer Rabbit only sat down and steered at the stern. Brer Bear, with his back to him, did not know this.

'Oh, my poor aching back!' he groaned.

'Aw, stop moaning,' said Brer Rabbit. 'Let's think of a sure way of getting him!'

Ten minutes of solid thinking gave Brer Rabbit an idea. It will work, he decided, and that would leave Brer Anansi stranded on the island!

'Listen,' he explained to Brer Bear. 'We take the hamper out and that did make the boat lighter. Then we paddle quickly up the creek, stop where Brer Anansi left his boat, and we tow it away. Before he knows what is what, he'll be alone on the island with no boat to return in!'

Brer Bear shook his head. 'I don't like your plan,' he said. 'Why?'

'Because we will be leaving our food hamper on the island.'

'Oh, you stupid Brer Bear!' exclaimed Brer Rabbit. 'We will collect it on our way out of the creek!'

'Then why didn't you say so in the first place?' said Brer Bear. 'You really had me worried.'

Brer Rabbit eyed him awhile and then continued. 'If I know Brer Anansi, he will leave his hamper in the boat and go look for a nice picnic spot. That way, we did be having two lunch baskets. There did be more to eat!'

'Ah!' Brer Bear licked his lips. 'Now you are talking sense! Come on. Let's go get the boat!'

They left their basket on the island, just at the head of the creek and proceeded to where they thought Brer Anansi was. Meanwhile, their lunch basket had floated: Brer Bear had been so excited that he had not placed it properly on the bank. Neither of the friends realized it!

Brer Anansi, in the meantime, had not found a suitable picnic spot. He decided to come out of the creek and go and look around the other side of the island. While coming out, he had no idea that his two enemies were coming in, full speed. There was a bend in the creek and he could not see the river.

As luck would have it, Brer Bear happened to look down in the clear water. He saw Brer Rabbit's reflection clearly. He was most shocked! Brer Rabbit was not paddling at all!

Brer Bear too stopped paddling. Slowly, sure enough, the boat came to a stop some yards into the creek.

'Come on, Brer Bear,' urged Brer Rabbit. 'Can't we go faster? Why have you stopped?'

Brer Bear turned around to face Brer Rabbit. 'I know

what your game is, you rascal! Tricking me! I am not paddling any more! You paddle now and I will steer!'

Brer Rabbit could not agree to that. Oh, no! He seized his paddle by the handle and swished it about.

'Either you leave now or paddle!' he threatened. 'This is my boat!'

'Your boat?' asked Brer Bear. 'You must be crazy! Who helped you tar it last year, the year before and still the year before?' And he too seized an oar and threatened to push Brer Rabbit off the boat!

Brer Anansi rounded the bend and was amazed to see a full-scale battle of oars and paddle going on! Swat! Swat! Swat! Swish! Blat! Whap! Whap!

'Yeow!'

'Take that! And that! And another!' Swish!

'Yeow!' Swat!

'Take it back!' Swish! Swish! Swat!

Brer Anansi slowly paddled his way up to his two enemies. What did he care? It was their battle, not his! Just as he was about to pass the rocking boats, Brer Rabbit spotted him.

'There! Brer Anansi!' he shouted. 'He's leaving! Grab the boat!'

He lunged for the boat and only managed to get hold of the tow-rope. He could not hold on to it and it swished out of his hands as if it had grease on it. The force of the swish sent the hook flying, and it narrowly missed Brer Anansi's head. Brer Anansi did not wait to pull the rope in. He was eager to be off before they sank his boat.

Brer Bear's oar, meanwhile, had knocked out the water cork at the bow of the boat. Water was coming in fast!

'Bail! Bail!' shouted Brer Rabbit. 'Bail or we'll sink!'

They both bailed away but it was useless! The water was

107

sure coming in faster than they could bail it out. Brer Rabbit noticed more water coming in. He turned to Brer Bear who had moved into the stern.

'What are you doing?'

Brer Bear tossed the stern cork into the water. 'I've made another hole. The water will come in that one and go out this one.'

'Oh no!' groaned Brer Rabbit. 'Look what you've done! Now the boat will sink faster, you great oaf of a blockhead!'

'Eh?' Brer Bear scratched his head. 'I thought—'

'Never mind what you thought. The trouble with you is that you never *think*! Quick, head for where you left the lunch basket! We might just make it!'

They both paddled the short distance. This time Brer Rabbit was paddling madly! He did not feel like a swim that morning. They reached the mouth of the creek and the boat stuck itself into the mud at the bank of the creek. Only three inches of the boat was showing at the top of the water.

They both stared at Brer Anansi's boat. It was almost out of sight. It was no use shouting after him for a lift home!

Then Brer Bear noticed that the lunch basket was missing.

'The basket!' he shouted. 'Just where is the basket!' They both looked around.

'There!' exclaimed Brer Rabbit, pointing at the back of Brer Anansi's boat. 'He has gone with it!' The flying hook at the end of Brer Anansi's tow-rope had caught the handle of Brer Rabbit's food basket and Brer Anansi was tugging it without even realizing!

How the two friends shouted at Brer Anansi to bring back the basket! But it was useless. Brer Anansi was too far away to help. He could not hear a thing!

The two friends would have to wait until the tide went out, and then they would cork up both holes with mud and pieces of their clothing. Then they waited until the tide came in again and floated the boat. It took them a long time and they couldn't get home until it was dark. Probably even early next morning. How Brer Rabbit regretted having interfered with Brer Anansi! He was feeling sad and hungry, and so was his friend Brer Bear, who was almost asleep with exhaustion.

Brer Anansi went home. He didn't really know what had happened, but he knew that if he stayed on the island his enemies would give him no peace. He decided to go home and have his picnic. Indeed, there was no way he could hear his enemies' shouts because he had stopped up his ears with pieces of his handkerchief as soon as he had left the jetty!